How had she gotten herself into such a mess?

All she needed was a place to hide. Why couldn't he compromise? Why was he holding her so close, and why was she suddenly so aware of the heat of his hand on her hip?

Obviously he had no concerns for *her* welfare. He thought only of his children. But then, what had she expected? She'd known Craig Banks's reputation.

What she hadn't expected was her own reaction to his proximity, a nameless silvery excitement that tensed every muscle and scattered her senses.

As he carried her up the stairs, panic clutched her. Somehow she'd lost control of the situation. "Where are you taking me?"

His eyes gleamed. "To bed."

ABOUT THE AUTHOR

Susan Kearney likes suspense-packed romance with an unforgettable twist. She's also more than fond of feisty heroines and heroes with soft hearts and hard heads. Sue lives in Florida with her husband, two children and two Boston terriers.

Books by Susan Kearney

HARLEQUIN INTRIGUE

Don't miss any of our special offers. Write to us at the following address for information on our newest releases.

Harlequin Reader Service
U.S.: 3010 Walden Ave., P.O. Box 1325, Buffalo, NY 14269
Canadian: P.O. Box 609, Fort Erie, Ont. L2A 5X3

Deceiving Daddy
Susan Kearney

Harlequin Books

TORONTO • NEW YORK • LONDON
AMSTERDAM • PARIS • SYDNEY • HAMBURG
STOCKHOLM • ATHENS • TOKYO • MILAN
MADRID • WARSAW • BUDAPEST • AUCKLAND

For Mom, who encouraged my dreams
and cheered my success.

ISBN 0-373-22456-7

DECEIVING DADDY

Copyright © 1998 by Susan Kearney

CAST OF CHARACTERS

Summer Warren—On the run from a stalker, Summer's last hope of survival hinges on the irresistible man she has lied to.

Craig Banks—A man whose life takes an alluring and dangerous twist once he marries Summer by proxy.

Gran—Summer's grandmother who tries to protect her.

Kendrick Yarlboro—Summer's egocentric ex-boyfriend. How far will he go to get her back?

Fred Hardcastle—A family friend. But can Summer count on him?

Harry Pibbs—The family's attorney and Summer's former boss. Did he know more about her parents' estate than he was admitting?

Bob Carlson—Summer's great uncle. Is he a keeper of old secrets or confused by alcohol-induced delusions?

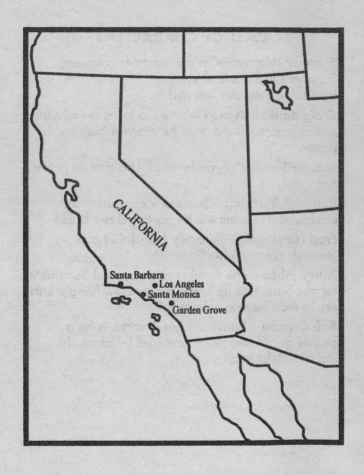

Prologue

Her sense of impending danger kicked in with no warning, just an ominous prickle on the back of her neck. Every day this week she'd spent her lunch hour in the park beside the lake, and every day the ducks gobbled the bread until not a crumb remained.

Until today.

Heads bobbing and weaving, the gaggle fluttered their wings and drew closer together as if sensing a threat.

Impossible. She was safe now.

She tossed the last crumbs and looked around. Nervousness stayed with her.

The kids celebrating their last days of summer freedom before school began skated by and disappeared, as had the mothers pushing baby strollers and the men reading the *Santa Del Ray Times* on wooden park benches. The breeze picked up, rustling the oak branches. Scudding clouds blocked the California sun, leaving her with a sudden chill sprinting up her spine.

Jamming her fists into her jacket pockets, she turned away from the lake. She tried to convince herself she was only imagining a threat. Tried to ignore the hair on the back of her neck standing on end. Tried to breathe evenly, although her breath lodged in her throat.

At the roar of an engine firing up, her heart tripped against her ribs. Motorcycles weren't allowed in the park.

Don't panic. He isn't coming for me.

She increased her pace along the sidewalk that encircled the lake, staying clear of the broken slat fence by the bicycle paths.

Take it easy.

Just because someone was taking an afternoon joyride didn't mean he was after her again.

Did it?

The bike emerged from behind a grassy hill. Dressed in black leather from head to foot, the rider twisted his wrist and revved the motor. A dark helmet with an opaque face shield prevented her from discerning his features.

He lifted his boot from where he had it braced and steered toward her. Maybe he only wanted to ask directions?

No.

She hadn't bolted three steps before he blocked her path. Willing her knees not to buckle, she sidestepped the bike.

From his boot, he extracted a baton. With a flick of his hand, the baton extended and locked in place with an ominous click.

Once again, a sick, trapped feeling threatened to corner her. She couldn't outrun a motorcycle. And no one would hear her scream.

He beat his leather-gloved palm with the baton,

then raised it over her head. He meant to kill her. To him, her life wasn't worth much. But she had so much to lose.

Cold resolve steeled her spine. She wasn't ready to die. Or stand still like a sheep in a slaughterhouse.

When he swung the baton at her head, she lunged forward, slammed into him, and man, woman and machine tumbled in a tangle of flesh and metal.

She landed on top of the pile, the wind knocked out of her. The bike pinned him in the dirt. As she scrabbled to rise and fill her lungs, she fumbled for the ignition key. Serrated metal bit into her palm.

Run.

She darted out of the park. Over the pounding of her heart, she listened for footfalls behind her but heard nothing above the roaring in her ears. She broke through the trees and careered into a policeman at the corner hot-dog stand.

Oh, thank God...

She and the officer returned to the park, but only the bike remained. Her attacker had escaped. She swallowed her tears, frustrated she still didn't know his identity.

This time, he'd let her see him. This time, he'd gotten so close. Next time, she might not be so lucky. It was time to put her plan into action.

She cradled her hand over her belly.

Time to disappear.

Chapter One

Of all the mornings for some idiot to roar up his driveway.

Craig Banks had been awake thirty-six hours straight, and he'd anticipated a good ten hours of sleep. Undisturbed. Negotiating the last kinks out of the Taiwan-Singapore contracts vital to keeping his company afloat had used up the last of his energy and patience. Yet from the sound of the revving motor below, he now had to deal with some motorcycle maniac lost in his driveway.

Welcome back to L.A. Apparently, living in the suburbs no longer guaranteed a peaceful morning.

Tossing off the tangled sheet, he yanked on a pair of jeans. Without bothering with shirt or shoes, he charged downstairs and flung open the double-wide front door. Whatever invective he'd been about to hurl died in his throat.

He'd expected a punk kid skidding doughnuts on his manicured lawn, not a fantasy woman in black leather, climbing off a motorcycle. But she was real—no fantasy conjured up from a mind lacking sleep. From her booted heels, trim ankles and legs that angled all the way up to curvy hips, she was dressed to drive a man wild. Although she wore a helmet, there could be no doubt of her gender, not with the leather clinging seductively to her lithe curves. Nothing lithe about her chest, though. Her breasts were high and firm, swelling out of a low-scooped neckline.

She removed her helmet, and a lion's mane of waist-length curly red hair tumbled down her back and sprang around her face, framing bright green eyes, a pert nose and hot-red lips. At any moment, he expected her to break into song and dance and a strip-tease.

Only it wasn't his birthday.

She smiled at him, a smooth, sexy smile that tied his stomach in knots and reminded him it had been too long since he'd been with a woman. Of course, hot-blooded redheads in black leather weren't his type, no matter how seductive. His preference ran to blondes, short, sophisticated blondes who had graduated from Radcliffe or Stanford and who never reminded him of his wife. Linda had been a redhead.

He threaded his fingers through his hair, in no mood for adolescent pranks or for memories that caused so much pain. "What do you want?"

He'd used a tone that quelled his employees, but she advanced like a stalking lioness, never breaking stride. She didn't stop until she stood so close he caught a whiff of vanilla. The delicate scent seemed so at odds with the rest of her that he studied her more closely. If he hadn't seen uncertainty flicker across her face before she straightened her spine, planted her fists on trim hips and stared him squarely in the eye, he'd have thought her invulnerable.

"Answer me, woman. What do you want?"

"Is that any way to greet your wife?" she asked, her voice a throaty purr.

He cocked a brow. "Wife? My wife is dead."

She ignored his quizzical expression. "Do I look dead? I'm wife number two."

A shudder ripped through him and he fought the strong urge to run like hell. If she *was* his wife—the one he'd wed by proxy—she was the last person he wanted to see.

His fingers tightened on the doorjamb while he dredged the specifics of their bargain from his memory. Their contract was straightforward. Strictly business. He paid expenses. If she delivered, he'd honor the balance. Although he couldn't recall the small print, her showing up on his doorstep damned sure wasn't part of their agreement.

Their arrangement, if successful, wouldn't end for another eight months. Still, he preferred to forget their marriage. When he thought of the woman at all, he pictured her as faceless, colorless, shapeless. Imagining her seductive curves hugged by sexy black leather or envisioning her brilliant green eyes meeting his with a sassy expression had never crossed his mind.

He scowled. Better keep to business.

To deal with her, he'd have to find out if she really *was* his wife. He studied her vivid features, telling himself to tread warily. Purposely, he let his gaze drift over her. The slight shifting of her weight indicated she wasn't as cool and calm as she first appeared, but with a determined look she kept her chin high.

What was she up to? How had she found him? She must already want more money.

He had opened his mouth to tell her to leave when she leaned closer, her breasts inches from his chest, the scent of leather enticing him. "I am your wife and I'm feeling fine, thank you. And very much alive."

Indulging in a look at the enticing shadow of a deep cleft between her breasts, he cleared his throat. "I can *see* that."

He hadn't expected her to blush. She hadn't seemed the type. Nor did he expect to find the blush so attractive. He was bleary-eyed tired, but he'd have to be dead not to respond to her combination of overt sensuality and blushing naiveté. But something was wrong. Her innocent demeanor contrasted too vividly with her bold and sexy outfit.

"Stay right there," he ordered, backing away but leaving the door open to keep an eye on her. Fleeing as much to search for the file on his "wife" as to hide his all-too-obvious physical reaction to her, he strode into the den. Still groggy but with morose foreboding, he recalled a picture somewhere.

Dean, Atherson, and Jackson were nothing if not thorough. His attorneys had checked the woman's background before he'd consented to the proxy marriage. Craig had a picture of his wife in the file and he didn't remember a red bombshell but a dull brunette. With a muttered curse, he stalked into his home office, jerked open the door that hid his storage cabinet and seized a handful of folders.

He flung aside the superfluous files in search of the one he wanted. Smith, Temple, Warren...

Got it.

As he returned, he reached into the folder, then scowled at a fuzzy photo of a, sure enough, mousy brunette. He squinted in frustration as he compared the blurred features to the vibrant woman who'd entered his foyer with the boldness of a vamp.

She carried a duffel slung over her shoulder and headed blithely toward the den, her hips swaying seductively in tight black leather. Where was she going? Seething with mounting irritation at his limited options, he approached her, glancing at the picture he held and then back to her. She *did* resemble the woman he'd married.

"Just a minute." He wasn't president and sole owner of an up-and-coming international corporation for nothing. He knew how to make executive questions sound like a threat. Gritting his teeth, he pointed, his finger stopping just short of the recess between her heaving breasts. "Just what in hell do you think you're doing?"

She started at the leashed violence in his tone, then cocked her chin at a jaunty angle. "I'm moving in."

"What!"

Then again, his university professors had often told him he wasn't cut of executive material.

"Don't yell at me."

She glared at him as if she had every right to live with him. If he hadn't been so annoyed, he might have admired her for standing up to him. No one else did, not his vice presidents, nor his salesmen. Certainly not a slip of a female.

Yet, instead of retreating, she stretched to her full height, squared her shoulders and advanced to stand toe-to-toe with him. "Hasn't anyone told you it's not healthy to upset a pregnant woman?"

"Hasn't anyone told you it's not healthy for a pregnant woman to ride a motorcycle?" he countered, his gut gripping tight at the unnecessary risks she'd taken. "Especially when you're carrying *my* children."

"I may be carrying your babies, but that doesn't mean you can run my life."

That did it. Fury rose up to choke him. Even worse, he could no longer deny she was his wife. He would have cheerfully sold a chunk of his soul to avoid having had to use a surrogate. Having a choice wasn't one of his options.

Ever since he'd decided to hire a surrogate, he'd worried over his lack of control during the pregnancy. If the surrogate chose to drink herself into a stupor, take up skydiving or experiment with drugs while carrying his children, he had no right to stop her. So he'd had his attorney select the best candidate and done his damnedest not to think about the dangers. Now she had the nerve to show up here and throw the fact that he couldn't protect his babies in his face.

Every muscle coiled into a tight spring of tension. "If you don't like my tone, I suggest you leave before I do something worse."

"Like what?" A defiant challenge angled across full lips that he found all too inviting.

His mouth watered, and he suddenly recognized the baffling cauldron of emotion bubbling inside him wasn't just anger. Sure, he was vexed, annoyed and outraged by her audacity—but he was also turned on.

He ought to kiss her senseless. Unbidden images of tasting her lush lips taunted him, tantalized him almost enough to make him pursue her. Almost.

The fantasy couldn't quite quell his need to shake some sense into her. Instead, he clenched his fists in an effort to override his masculine reaction to her stirring old memories better left alone.

At the uncomfortable feeling in his gut, the sudden need to send her away almost overwhelmed him. Grasping the duffel, he tossed it from the foyer onto the front porch. "You aren't moving in. That wasn't part of our agreement."

With a new wariness in her eyes, she planted her hand on one hip and edged toward the kitchen. "Our agreement is going to change."

What game was she playing? Her apprehension was genuine enough even if she was careful to conceal it behind a thick layer of outward composure. The contradiction between her sassy words and the troubled look in her eyes made him wonder if she had something to hide.

He sensed reminding her of their legally binding contract would make no difference in her demented decision to live with him. She obviously wasn't a businesswoman and probably didn't understand the agreement she'd signed. Driven by frustration and forced to shift position to block her from gaining farther access into his home, he didn't bother to mask his irritation. "Why is that?"

"Since I've agreed to serve as a surrogate mother and bear your twins, I've done a lot of research."

He caught the tension and a hint of desperation in her tone and momentarily regretted his unwillingness to at least listen to her story. "What kind of research?"

"How to make babies."

At her saucy suggestiveness, he whistled and allowed his features to soften for a moment. "Most girls learn that before their teens."

He might not like the fact he'd gone from angry to interested in the space of a heartbeat, but now that he'd recognized his own response to her, he could deal with it—even if he was enjoying their confrontation too damn much. But would his plan work? He grinned, hoping blatant sexual suggestions would scare her into running right out the door and leaving him in peace.

Deliberately, he lowered his voice to a murmur. "If you're not sure how babies are made, I'd be willing to instruct you."

Her eyes widened, and her soft intake of air revealed she wasn't as sophisticated as she appeared. She looked down and studied her hands for a moment, then replied as if she'd never hesitated. "I'm not talking about sex. I'm talking about pregnancy. Did you know a fetus recognizes its parents' voices while still in the womb?"

She was one stubborn woman. He ought to pick her up, throw her over his shoulder and carry her out the front door. Yet the idea of running his hands along her curves was all too appealing.

Inadvertently, he stepped back. His mouth tightened in a grim line. "The point being?"

As if knowing the farther she advanced, the harder

it would be for him to kick her out, she stepped closer to the kitchen. "I can't grow the twins for you like peas in a pod and then just hand them over."

Her frosty words doused his seduction attempts as effectively as an icy shower. A warning shiver prickled down his spine, chilling him to the bone. If she thought for one moment she could change their contract and keep his kids, she had a shock coming. That's why he'd insisted on marrying the surrogate. Those babies were his, genetically *and* legally. "Explain yourself."

"You have to bond with your babies."

"Lady—"

"My name is Summer."

"I don't think—"

"Just talk to your babies. The softer you make your tone, the better." She cocked her head at a saucy angle while the underlying sincerity of her expression captivated him and threw him off balance at the same time. "Perhaps you can sing?"

He couldn't have heard her right. Confusion filtered through his wariness and he gulped. "Sing?"

"Since I'm moving in here, you'll be close enough for your children to become accustomed to your voice. If you sing to them, you can bond while they're still in the womb."

"That's ridiculous."

"I know it's early in the pregnancy. But the babies will sense your tone. They feel vibrations." Without warning, she took his hand and placed it over her womb.

He went completely still. The warmth of the life inside her radiated through the leather into his palm, filling him with unexpected wonder and banishing the chill. His babies were there. His children.

He'd never thought of the surrogate in terms of living, warm flesh. Her surprise move had robbed him of his emotional detachment, and he could no longer keep his accustomed and comfortable distance. He wanted to hate feeling this way. He didn't want to feel at all. It had been a long time since he'd allowed anyone to penetrate the echoes of the past and the wall he'd built around himself. But these were his babies. She was the woman who would bear his children.

Reeling with the knowledge that she wasn't simply a womb for hire but an individual with needs and desires and thoughts that could affect him and his children in the most profound ways, he fought down surging panic. By coming here, she'd personalized a service that was supposed to have been anonymous. She'd shattered his illusion of control. Suddenly, he felt as if he'd been caught in a nightmare from which he couldn't awaken.

Needing control of every faculty, he strode into the kitchen, aimed for the sink and turned on the faucet. With a springy bounce, she followed and stood watching. Ignoring her, he waited for the water to turn colder.

Leaning against the far counter, she wore a look of faint bemusement. "What are you doing?"

He didn't answer. When the spray numbed his fingers, he splashed his face, praying he'd awaken his sluggish mind to deal with her abrupt invasion into his life. He'd hoped he'd never have to meet her. He hadn't wanted to see her face, hear her voice, or

worse, breathe her enticing scent. He sure as hell
didn't want to touch her stomach, know details about
her pregnancy, or consider if it would be hard for her
to give up the babies.

He'd intended to remain aloof. In his mind, this
was just one more business deal. Now she wanted
them to live together. She wanted him to sing, damn
her.

She chuckled, the low contralto pleasant to his ears.
"You'll get used to me."

"That remains to be seen." Thoughts racing, he
splashed his face with icy water, then dried with a
clean dish towel. He didn't want her here in Linda's
house. He didn't want to get used to her. Yet she
carried his and Linda's children in her womb, and he
couldn't shake the certainty that his wishes were now
irrelevant. Why couldn't this Summer Warren surrogate go back to wherever she'd come from and let
him retreat to his comfortable bubble of isolation?

As long as she carried his children, he had few
alternatives. He couldn't risk alienating her. Despite
all his precautions, he had no wish to fight over the
children in court. Even worse, she could disappear
and he'd never again see her or his children. She
could be as demanding as she liked, and as if she'd
held a gun to his head, he'd be compelled to put up
with her. Unless he convinced her to leave, he was
stuck with a woman whom he found too damned
sexy, and if he guessed right, in trouble up to her
pretty little neck.

As he reared back and shut off the faucet, Summer
took an involuntary step back but fought her immediate reaction to pivot and run. Craig raked fingers

through his black hair while he scowled at her with grim determination. Not even a few stray water droplets spiking his lashes could soften his sharp cheekbones, arrogant jaw or the muscle flexing in his neck. Doing her best to ignore his chest, bronzed and bare except for a light dusting of hair, she kept her gaze locked with his. But when he hooked a thumb in his jeans, diverting her attention to the top button that remained unfastened, her mouth went dry.

Her gaze skimmed his features, noting the fatigue in dark eyes that glittered icily. His stubbornly squared chin portrayed the force of his personality, and only the full, sensuous lips hinted at any emotion but raw anger burning just below the surface.

As he tried to steamroller her with his harsh look, she refused to let his turbulent expression squash her determination. She'd blown the first impression big time.

While the disguise had been useful, the black leather clothing had been a mistake. He'd jumped to the wrong conclusion about her principles. She shouldn't blame him for thinking she sought to take advantage of him by moving in, since that's exactly what she was doing. But in this case, keeping the babies safe justified her outrageous, uncharacteristic and blatantly sexy behavior.

The black leather had made her feel sleazy, deceptive and out-of-her-league sexy. If she'd had another even half-decent choice, she would have taken it. However, she was out of options. Desperation had driven her to masquerade as a tease, and the ruse had worked. Although the heat in his eyes at the sight of her biker outfit made her wonder if she'd be safer on her own.

But alone, she was vulnerable. She told herself she would have insisted on living with Craig even if he'd had a live-in girlfriend. Yet she'd done her homework. The secretaries at Dean, Atherson, and Jackson gossiped incessantly. Collecting information about him without attracting notice hadn't been difficult. He didn't have a girlfriend, dating only occasionally since his wife's death.

A month ago, a glimpse of him walking through the office hallway had transfixed her. She'd found herself attuned to every remark she heard about him. But it wasn't his dark good looks, or his moderate wealth, or his house in a good neighborhood that drew her. That he'd lost his wife so young tugged at her heart. That he intended to raise the children alone had amazed and fascinated her. That he was so obviously available and handsome to boot made her distinctly uncomfortable, but she had more important things to dwell on than her attraction to Craig.

"You can't live here." His tone was cold, commanding.

Survival was her first priority. He had to let her stay. But she couldn't tell him she had nowhere else to go, so instead, she ignored the churning in her stomach and summoned a sweet smile. "Please, don't use that holier-than-thou tone. You don't want to scare your children, do you?"

All but snarling with temper, he folded his arms across his chest. "You're pregnant all of one month. My children aren't developed enough to have ears yet." He took a deep breath, his chest expanding.

Slowly, he expelled the air and spoke in a more reasonable tone. "Your moving in here isn't part of our agreement. It's not as if you don't have a place to live. With the funds I'm supplying to see you through this pregnancy, you could rent a penthouse apartment."

In the face of his bleak gray eyes, the cheery kitchen mocked her. If only she could tell him she needed his protection instead of misleading him. But she didn't dare. No matter how contemptible her little act, it was necessary to convince him to take her in.

Anger toward the stalker choked her. He'd disrupted her life for the second time, forcing her to lie through her teeth, steal a motorcycle and become adept at disguises to visit her grandmother. She'd had to drop her night classes at the law school she attended and she could ill afford the expense to retake them.

How far would she have to go to stay alive? Sexy hadn't worked. Perhaps it was time for tears.

It wasn't hard to squeeze a few out, not after her day. With her life once again in danger, she'd been forced to abandon her car. To flee, she'd taken the only other transportation available—the motorcycle. After she produced the motorcycle's ignition key and claimed the bike was hers, the officer had let her off with a warning not to ride in the park. That had been the least of her worries. She'd had to get away. Fast.

Thankful for the high school boyfriend who had taught her how to ride a motorcycle, she'd driven straight to the bus station. She'd checked the saddlebags, hoping for a clue to her stalker's identity. Instead, she'd found and appropriated the too-tight black leather clothes and helmet, retrieved her duffel from a locker where she'd also had the forethought to stash cash for emergencies. Even disguised in the flaming red wig, she hadn't dared to return to her apartment.

Until today, she'd thought her fortune had changed and that she'd eluded the stalker who'd persisted in pursuing her for months. In her former identity, she was supposed to have been safe. She had changed apartments and job, disguised her appearance and avoided her former hangouts.

Now, her cover blown, she sniffled and tried to appear helpless in the face of Craig's daunting anger. He had to buy her act. Didn't he have a heart behind that bare chest? A soul beneath those hard eyes?

The diamond edge in his gaze never lost its sharpness. Playing on his sympathy was a waste of time. The story about bonding with his babies was easier to believe than the truth—and he hadn't bought the story. Nor was he buying her tears. Time for another change in tactics.

From across the kitchen, he glared at her with suspicion. She hiccuped. "I don't feel so good."

Suiting action to words, she slid down the slick cabinet onto the ceramic tile. Three full strides carried him to her. With leashed power, he gathered her into his arms, lifting her as easily as if she were a child. Off balance, she let out a cry and threw her arms around his neck.

His laughter didn't curtail his stormy expression. "So, have I finally got you where you want to be?"

He'd asked his question in a manner as playful as a kid holding his first puppy. Then she glanced into eyes as darkly gray as thunderclouds on a summer's day, and her throat tightened. His warm breath fanned her neck and suddenly she realized he wasn't angry with her. A languid smile curving his lips, he'd dropped his gaze to her mouth and looked as if he was planning a gourmet meal. Did he think she owed him a little something if he agreed to let her stay? Another shiver racked her despite the heat of his bare shoulder against her cheek.

How had she gotten herself into such a mess? All she needed was a place to hide. She wouldn't get in his way. Why couldn't he compromise? Why was he holding her so close, and why was she suddenly so aware of the heat of his hand on her hip?

"Put me down."

A teasing smile played across his lips, yet his eyes remained hard, hinting of ulterior motives. "I don't think so. You look pale, unsteady, overwrought. I can't take a chance on your keeling over and injuring my children."

Obviously, he had no concerns for *her* welfare. But then what had she expected? Going in, she'd known Craig Banks's reputation—tough, uncompromising, adamantly single since his wife's death four years ago. What she hadn't expected was her own reaction to his proximity, a nameless, silvery excitement that tensed every muscle and scattered her senses.

He carried her out of the kitchen and up a sweeping flight of stairs without breathing hard. Taking the opportunity to study him, she realized he looked different up close. In his lawyer's office dressed in a suit and tie, with his hair combed, he'd appeared more civilized. Right now, from the slashing line of his mouth to the tensing muscle of his jaw, he reminded her of a savage.

As he carried her up the stairs, his shoulders rippling into a mountain of chest muscles, panic clutched her. Somehow she'd lost control of the situation. "Where are you taking me?"

"To bed." His eyes gleamed with a brief flash of amusement that she found irritating and insulting. And undeniably intriguing.

She'd made a fine mess of her situation. And Craig seemed more than willing to take advantage.

Her heart pounded so hard, that her ribs ached. "This isn't funny."

"Funny isn't what I have in mind."

She didn't need to ask what he did have in mind. The searing intensity in his eyes made her want to hide. Heat curled in her stomach.

From his teasing tone, he knew she was perfectly fine. He'd turned the tables on her, using her excuse of an illness to keep her in his arms. "Let me go."

He raised an eyebrow. "You'll leave?"

Damn him for calling her bluff.

"I can't."

"Well then, why shouldn't we enjoy ourselves?" He eyed her speculatively. "It's not as if we have to worry you'll become pregnant."

She didn't laugh at his humor. Unable to decide whether he was trying to intimidate her into leaving or really meant to take her to bed, she opted to let an uncomfortable silence express her indignation at his suggestion.

The twinkle in his eyes indicated he might be playing games. Yet she was all too aware of his thumb caressing her hip, his bold gaze lingering on her mouth and the maddening hint of arrogance in his tone that revealed he was aware of her reaction to him.

While she had no idea how she'd allowed the situation to veer so far out of control, she wouldn't be reduced to trading her body for a place to stay. She had to stop him before they reached the upper hallway and his bedroom. After a glance through the window behind him, she broke the taut silence by uttering the first thing she could think of to distract him. "There's a policeman in your driveway."

"Uh-huh." He looked at her as though she'd just escaped the insane asylum.

She shrugged. "Fine. Don't believe me."

As he turned at the top of the stairs, she peered again through the floor-to-ceiling windows of the two-story foyer. A police car, blue lights flashing, still stood in the driveway.

At least he'd have to put her down.

For once, she wished she'd been lying about the cop. Dealing with Craig's amorous advances was preferable to answering a policeman's questions. Through the foyer window, she watched a uniformed officer ring the front bell. At the chime, she stiffened and Craig turned.

She wriggled in an effort to make him put her down. "Have you forgotten I can walk?"

Ignoring her struggle except for a slight tightening of his arms, he shook his head. "I don't know when to believe you."

"I don't lie," she protested, wishing she spoke the

truth, wishing the masculine scent of him didn't intensify her rapid breathing.

He shot her a cool, calculating look. "Really? Something tells me otherwise. There's a cop at my front door and suddenly you're squirming. Keeping you from running seems like a very good idea."

She twisted, but for all the good her struggling did, his arms might have been carved of granite. "But—"

"I've never had a police officer come looking for me. Instinct tells me he wants to speak to you."

Finally, he put her down but kept a firm grip on her arm as they walked down the stairs and through the foyer.

Craig opened the door. "Come in."

A young, blue-eyed, blond-haired officer stepped inside. He grinned when he caught sight of her. "Sorry to disturb your day—"

"It's already been more than disturbed," Craig muttered while she fought not to fidget.

"Is the bike out front yours, sir?"

Craig's gray eyes drilled her with a piercing stare. "I believe the vehicle belongs to my wife."

The tension in Craig's hand radiated disapproval up her arm, and she swallowed hard. She'd intended to ditch the bike or hide it in his garage. In retrospect, she shouldn't have taken it. But she'd been running for her life. Returning to her car had been out of the question. What could she say?

"Is that true, ma'am? Do you own that bike?"

"Not exactly." A sinking sensation roiled deep in her stomach as she suspected her limited knowledge of the law wasn't enough to save her. But she couldn't let them lock her up—not with her grand-mother depending on Summer's visits.

Craig raised his eyes to the ceiling in disgust at her evasive reply. "What's the problem, Officer?"

"I know you leave the country often, sir. I didn't know you were back. When I saw a strange vehicle outside, I thought a robbery might be in progress. So I ran a make on the plates."

Craig gripped her tightly. "And?"

"The bike's stolen."

Chapter Two

The cop's statement hit Craig like a sucker punch to the jaw. He'd suspected Summer had secrets, perhaps a few unpaid parking tickets, but he hadn't guessed the surrogate so carefully screened by his attorneys could be a thief. Reeling, he backed away, hoping the distance between them would help him understand. It didn't.

As he waited for her explanation, a denial, an excuse, the remaining heat where she'd cuddled against his chest slowly cooled. His temper didn't.

She remained silent, her face pale. She wouldn't meet his eyes, either, but stared at a spot in the vicinity of his left shoulder.

"I'm afraid I'll have to ask you to come downtown, ma'am," the officer told her.

Unwilling to let her out of sight after this new revelation, Craig reached into his pocket for his car keys. "I'll drive her."

"If you gentlemen will excuse me, I'd like to change." Summer gestured to her black leather but directed her words at the cop. "My husband enjoys these kinds of games, but I should wear something more appropriate to court.''

More likely she was going to jail.

And that outfit had been strictly her idea. The conniving little witch was making him sound like some kind of pervert. He conveniently ignored the fact that he'd been alternately wildly furious and rashly attracted to her since she climbed off that bike. Or that he'd never again inhale the scent of leather without thinking of her.

She retrieved her duffel and walked past him with as much dignity as a woman dressed in black leather could muster. Her eyes still avoided his, and her bottom lip trembled.

Yet she lifted her chin defiantly. "While you calm down, dear, I'll change in the guest room."

Was that a not-so-subtle reminder that he needed at least to don a shirt? A hint that she'd moved in? Or her way of telling him she didn't intend to share his room?

For now.

Conflicting emotions stirred inside him, and compassion rose to the surface. What was it about her that made him want to help her and protect her? Her courage? The vulnerability she tried to hide? Or maybe he was rationalizing away the truth. While she carried his children, he didn't have a choice. Summer had already caused him more problems in the past hour than his first wife had during their five-year marriage. Were the memories of the terrible accident and the aching loss finally beginning to fade?

Of one thing he was certain. If Summer lived here, he could afford to be patient because eventually he'd make love to her. As his thoughts kept cartwheeling, he clapped a hand on his forehead. He must be crazy.

The birth mother of his children was a motorcycle mama. A thief. Even thinking of taking her to bed was out of the question. The shock of meeting Summer Warren must have fried his brain.

He had to get his act together. Pull some strings. Luckily, although his business profits had slipped during the years since he'd lost his wife, he was getting his company back on track. Besides, there wasn't a judge in town who didn't owe him a favor.

No matter how badly his lawyers had misled him in their search for a suitable surrogate to bear his children, his kids would *not* lack for fresh air and sunshine while she went to jail. Not if he had anything to say about it.

Planning on speaking to her, he bounded up the stairs three at a time but hesitated outside the guestroom door. Summer was talking, her voice low. "Gran, I may not be able to visit today. I've got to go downtown to the courthouse."

Ashamed that he'd been reduced to eavesdropping on her phone call, he strode down the hall and to his bedroom, kicked off his jeans and changed into business attire. He knotted his tie with automatic precision while his thoughts raced. At least today was a weekday and he stood a chance of arranging her release. He combed his hair and wondered which judge was sitting on the bench.

After returning downstairs, Craig gave the officer a soft drink while they waited for Summer. At the click of a high heel, the cop glanced up and choked.

Craig patted the man on the back, then pivoted to look up. "Summer?"

"Yes." The same throaty voice answered, but that was all he recognized, except for the incredibly long legs shown off by silk hose and heels. Shocked wide-awake, he stared.

The red mane of lioness hair was gone, replaced by a smooth, sophisticated honey gold ending just below her elegant diamond-studded earrings. She'd replaced the hot-red lipstick with a more natural color, exchanged the black leather for a soft gray-and-cream pin-striped power suit. Cream-colored lace peeked out of the vee of the jacket suitable for any attorney to wear to court. A delicate gold chain hung around her regal neck, an antique locket resting in the hollow of her throat.

She must have sensed his astonishment. Her mouth turned up in a haunting smile. With the serenity of a celebrity about to take her bow after a stellar performance, she offered him the crook of her arm. "This outfit will be more appropriate."

SUMMER DIDN'T HAVE to read minds to know Craig Banks's famous temper was about to explode in her direction. The tense grip on her arm as he dragged her out of the courthouse and down the steps into the sunshine amid the five-o'clock crowd on the city sidewalks never eased.

"That was some story you told the judge."

"I told the truth."

"Yeah, right."

She winced at his sarcastic tone. When the judge remanded her to her husband's custody, Craig's mouth had puckered as if he'd been chewing a bitter pill. Without glancing at her, he'd accepted the responsibility with a stiff nod. She couldn't blame him for his disgust at having to take charge of a criminal, for feeling used and betrayed. No doubt if he could now choose another surrogate, he would do so—and to keep the babies safe, she'd gladly give them up. But that wasn't possible.

If the babies were to survive, they had to remain inside her. And she needed his assistance to stay alive.

So where was the relief she'd expected to feel at attaining Craig's help? Convinced that accepting his leashed anger and ill-concealed censure was easier than telling him the truth, she endured the anxiety and tension in silence. Still, the irony of her situation mocked her.

If only she could run. But she couldn't leave Gran. So she was stuck with Craig Banks and he with her.

His expression cold and accusing, he turned to her at the foot of the courthouse steps. "Did you really expect Judge Thordale to believe your grandmother bought that stolen motorcycle?"

"Gran's a little senile," she lied. The woman who'd raised her was shrewd and as sharp as a Stanford graduate. Fortunately, her grandmother was also skillful at extemporizing, claiming mental gymnastics put a bit of excitement in an otherwise dull existence. More importantly, she'd know what to say if any cops arrived at the nursing home to ask questions. Even better, Garden Grove, the town where Gran lived, had a different police department than Santa Del Ray.

"Let's pay your grandmother a visit."

"Why?"

Craig didn't reply. Instead, he tightened his grip on her as if he feared she'd escape. He led her through the crowd, and her thoughts churned. Gran was good, but could she fool his acute perceptiveness? Summer had already learned Craig was adept at reading people. From his skeptical glances, she could clearly see *she* hadn't allayed his suspicions.

She and Gran would have to stay on guard or he'd trip them up. She frowned. Since Summer hadn't had time to fully explain that the stalker had found her again, would Gran pick up her cues?

At least Summer no longer had to worry about going to jail.

Because she had no prior record and because Craig had supported the judge's last campaign, she was now a free woman. Sort of. For a split second, she had the crazy urge to turn and thank him for standing beside her in court. Then she risked a glance at Craig's hard face and wondered if she'd have been better off in jail.

A muscle flexed in his jaw, and she canceled her absurd notion. Dressed in a suit and tie, he looked every inch the calm, cultured businessman, but the tight grip of his long fingers on her arm betrayed the fury seething beneath the controlled surface.

Nothing was going the way she'd planned. She was supposed to be holed up at home, comfortably curled on a sofa with a good book and munching on carrot sticks—not hiding from a killer. Instead, she was stuck with a keeper who didn't trust her, a husband who resented her, and a soon-to-swell belly. While her lies were tame compared to the truth, they were necessary to keep her safe.

If she died, so would the precious lives inside her. Even if it meant lying and stealing, the babies had to come first. Craig might not approve of her methods, but she had to protect his children. Nonetheless, the unsettling image of his probable reaction when she finally told him the truth had her trembling.

He marched her along the busy street, and she hurried to match his long stride, heels clicking madly to keep up. Men and women chattered as they exited office buildings. The crowds overflowed the sidewalks and spilled into the streets. As the throng rushed home to loved ones, Summer imagined hearts brimming with happiness, welcoming hugs and home-cooked meals.

In contrast, what probably awaited her was a lecture—that is, if he deigned to break his furious silence to speak to her.

After waiting for the light on the corner to turn green, Summer and Craig stepped off the curb to cross Granville, a busy four-way intersection. From her right, a white Mercedes raced through a red light.

The crowd scattered. A woman screamed. Brakes screeching, the car skidded and fishtailed her way.

No.

Her heart hammered. Her blood iced. He couldn't be after her again, not twice in one day.

Summer froze.

Craig's fingers tightened on her upper arm, jerked her aside. Out of harm's way. The car passed so close she could have touched the chrome bumper. At Craig's fierce tug, she crashed into him and would have crumpled if he hadn't cradled her against his chest to steady her. She clung to him, unable to stop the shudders that racked her. They could have been killed. Was no place safe?

"Get the license number," she gasped.

Brakes squealed and the sound of metal crunching drew her attention. She couldn't see. Around them, people panicked, a dog barked, a child cried. A bicyclist rode by as if nothing unusual had happened.

"Sorry. Too many people are in the way."

He stroked her back, comforting her. She should chase after the car, write down the license number. But she didn't want to give up the protective strength of his arms. For the first time in a long while, someone was worried about her, and relaxing against his broad chest felt undeniably good.

His former fury had been replaced by tight white lines of concern at the corners of his mouth. "Are you all right?"

Shaking, she nodded, leaning against the solid strength of him to remain upright on wobbly legs.

Would this never end?

He led her to the corner bus stop and carefully lowered her to a bench, his tone gentle. "You're pale. Put your head between your knees."

He nudged her head down, his warm hand cradling her neck with a tenderness she'd never suspected in him. She took deep, calming breaths until the light-headedness ceased.

As her fright eased, a sour taste rose up into her mouth. Surely the attacker in the park hadn't already found her? How could he have picked up her trail when she hadn't returned to her apartment or her car? His spotting her on the sidewalk could just have been her bad luck. But these clothes were nothing like her normal attire. Neither was the blond wig.

Damn it! She was supposed to have been protected and safe in this new identity.

"Do you want something to drink?"

She shook her head, unwilling to remain alone, hating the lie of omission this time. While he believed the close call an accident, she knew better.

Being unable to predict the stalker's next move left her at a disadvantage and she considered telling Craig the truth. In the face of his kindness, the burden of her secret had never weighed so heavily. But at the thought of facing the next eight months alone, her fear spiked, thoroughly stifling her desire to confess.

"I'll be okay. It's my hormones overreacting," she lied. "Just give me a minute."

Her nerves really were on edge. Yet Craig's solicitous concern revealed a side of him she hadn't known existed until now. Despite the fright, she liked his holding her close and fussing over her. Knowing his hands could comfort as well as suffuse her with heat jolted her to a painful awareness.

His concern's not for you but his children, the cynic in her scoffed.

Her hand moved protectively to her stomach.

"Are you okay?" Panic tinged his voice. "Should I find a doctor?"

"I'm all right. The babies are fine." Her hands trembled and she clenched them.

"You're shaking." Ignoring the dirt, he knelt on the sidewalk beside her, clasped her cold hands and rubbed them briskly between his warm ones. She wanted to hang on tight and never let go.

Easy. Get a grip. I'm safe now. Surely her attacker wouldn't try to run her over again right away.

Dizzy, she sat up and peered through the throng of people on the sidewalk. The white Mercedes had jumped the curb and crashed into a brick wall. Hope surged at the possibility her attacker might have been injured and caught.

She peered through the crowd gathered to gawk at the Mercedes. Unharmed thanks to an air bag, the driver was a woman!

Disappointment haunted her.

The driver wasn't her stalker. There was no way her attacker in the park could have been a woman. The motorcyclist whose bike she'd taken had broad shoulders, a flat chest and thick arms. Whoever he was, wherever he was, he was alive and well. Discouragement, sharp and bitter, left Summer even shakier.

Her blood stilled, infusing her bones with ice. The cold horror would never be vanquished—not until the man who'd tried to kill her was caught. On the other hand, this sidewalk incident was a simple accident. He hadn't found her again.

I'm safe. For the moment.

Though the concern on Craig's face was probably for his babies, his steady gray eyes searched hers with compassion. Obviously, he was a man capable of deep feelings. Powerful feelings.

All of them for his first wife and children, she reminded herself.

"Are you sure you're all right?"

"It's the hormones. Ever since the doctors implanted the embryos, I've been emotional, a normal result of pregnancy," she lied once more, unable to discern whether he believed her.

He didn't argue. Again she wished she could tell him the truth. She must be more shaken than she'd realized to consider confiding in him. Staying hidden was crucial, as much for her own safety as for his children's.

After her strength returned, he led her into the nearest coffee shop. The cheery red-and-white-checkered country decor derided her bleak mood. Her nerves jangled. Although she yearned for coffee, the caffeine wouldn't be good for the twins, so she ordered cranberry juice with a tuna sandwich.

Slowly, her nerves settled, and she munched absently. Opposite her, Craig's observant dark eyes measured her every move. Clearly, he was full of questions, and just as clearly, he wouldn't risk upsetting her.

His scrutiny, as if he feared she was about to break apart at any moment, made her uneasy. "You don't have to keep staring at me as if I'm going to fall apart. I'm stronger than I look."

"Sorry."

Fearing in her overwrought state, she might slip up, she didn't want to answer questions about herself. Right now, she wanted assurance she'd done the right thing by trusting this man. He certainly seemed concerned about his babies. She brushed her fingers over her stomach. "These children must mean a lot to you."

He stared at his half-eaten burger. "They mean everything to me."

"Most men don't choose to raise children alone. You must have loved your wife very much."

He nodded, then sipped his coffee, his starkly chiseled face giving away nothing.

"I don't want to make you uncomfortable, but I wondered, why now?" she persisted. "What made you go ahead after all these years?"

His eyes lowered as if to hide pain. He drained his mug and set it aside. "We always wanted children. After Linda's death, it just seemed right to carry on with her wishes."

Clearly, sorrow washed over him as he recalled his wife. Summer hesitated, wondering if she dared ask her next question, then plunged ahead. "How did she die?"

He didn't say it, but his eyes revealed he still carried the grief with him. Summer couldn't help but wonder what it would be like to have a man love her so deeply that his gaze mirrored the intensity of his devotion. She knew a bit more about him than she intended to admit. The fact she'd seen him before she'd keep strictly to herself.

Craig closed his eyes, looking totally miserable. Although his words were deceptively calm and devoid of emotion, a faint tremor shook him. "I lost her at the beach. She was caught in a riptide. A lifeguard and I finally pulled her out, but it was too late."

"I'm sorry."

"I should have known better than to swim with the waves cresting ten feet." Guilt and pain layered his razor-sharp tone. "Loving the water, Linda had insisted. I could never refuse her."

"You can't blame yourself."

"I still feel responsible for her death."

And it was obvious, he still missed her with all his heart. A fertility specialist had removed Linda's eggs and combined them in a laboratory with Craig's sperm. But Linda had died before the doctor could implant the embryos. During the four years the embryos had been frozen Craig had been unable to forget. The babies in Summer's womb were his last link to Linda. Part of her would live on through them, the promise of better days, of all their hopes and dreams. His deceased wife's presence was so strong at the moment, Summer felt as if Linda was silently rooting her on.

"My mother talked me into waiting to find a surrogate, believing that the grief should pass before I made such an important decision."

Perhaps he thought the children would make him whole. After the doctors at the clinic had given her background material about Craig, she'd become curious about a single man who still wanted to have his deceased wife's children. Her initial intention had been to give him the children he wanted so badly so his soul could be in peace.

"Mom thought I would meet another woman," he continued, "and she hoped I'd forget Linda and our wish for children, but..."

"But you never did," she finished for him. Her eyes brimmed, and she tried to swallow the lump in her throat. She couldn't help a twinge of envy. No one had ever loved her that much.

Unlike Craig, who had fond memories of wife and marriage, Summer's past had been more rocky. Although she and Kendrick Yarlboro had enjoyed several happy years, their relationship hadn't lasted. In the two years since their breakup, she hadn't been attracted to a man beyond casual interest.

"What about you?" he asked, a dangerous edge to his tone. "Why did you agree to bear children for a stranger?"

"You must have seen my profile." She had no wish to repeat the personal reasons she'd given to the psychologist before her application had been accepted. In the face of his honesty, grief and pain, he deserved the truth.

Guilt kept her silent.

The waitress left a check and he paid, leaving a generous tip. He made no move to leave. Instead, he went completely still under the harsh lights, his blunt-cut black hair gleaming. "You sure you can give up the children when the time comes?"

So, he'd finally asked the sixty-four-thousand-dollar question. She couldn't blame him for believing her a thief, for doubting her intentions. Yet she wanted to hate him for questioning whether she'd already changed her mind, wanted to despise him for thinking her so weak in character. Still, she couldn't hate him when *she* was the one who'd lied from the beginning and maintained the lie now.

At least this time, she could answer without hesitation. "You and Linda are the parents. I'm just the baby-sitter."

His majestic gray eyes bored into hers. "You're a lot more than a baby-sitter. You'll lose your figure, go through the pain of childbirth."

She grinned. "Not to mention morning sickness, heartburn and waddling like a duck."

He returned her grin, then with a puzzled expression, he furrowed his high forehead, arched his ebony brows and shoved his fingers through his hair. "What I'm paying you doesn't seem enough."

She hadn't agreed to be a surrogate for the money, but he would never believe that. Did he think she'd tracked him down to extract more money from him? If he was that cynical, he'd never believe how much she'd wanted children and that she'd given up hope of finding a man she wanted to marry in order to have them.

Even if she couldn't raise his kids, having them was her chance to do something good, to bring life into the world. She didn't expect a man to understand. Her motives were difficult to put into words. Her own mother hadn't lived to raise her, but Summer had always been grateful for her ultimate gift of life. Now she had her turn to pass the gift on.

Looking into his harsh features, she could never adequately explain such an abstract concept. Instead, she spoke of specifics. "Your terms are more than generous. But I'd prefer you take me in. I want to live with you. It'll be better for your babies."

She held her breath. If he booted her out now, she had nowhere to hide—and she and his unborn twins were as good as dead.

His lips curved into a wry smile that made him look carefree and boyish. "Bonding?"

She chuckled. "Bonding."

AFTER THEIR MEAL in the café, Craig escorted Summer to his car, gratified to see color had returned to her cheeks. In one fell swoop, he'd almost lost his children and he told himself that his concern for Summer was secondary. However, fear for her safety had heightened his curiosity. He now had more questions than before.

Who was she? Why was she so frightened?

Summer slipped into disguises with a practiced nonchalance, playing her roles with an adeptness he found alluring and all the more fascinating for her lack of perfection that allowed him glimpses of her true character. Recalling her in the provocative black leather and wild red hair had him wondering what she'd have done if he'd walked right up to her and kissed her full lips. Oddly, he found the demure suit and blond hair just as intriguing. What was happening to him? How had he let a liar and thief slip past his normal barriers?

When he held her trembling in his arms, his concern had been every bit as much for her welfare as the babies. That in itself told him how close she was to forcing him to look at how he'd been deceiving himself. Taking her to bed once or twice wouldn't be enough. Even if he could handle a one-nighter, she was too complex for a simple fling. Even if she wasn't, taking her to bed was too risky when he had so much to lose. He had to keep the babies' welfare firmly in the forefront of his mind.

If only she looked pregnant, he would have had an easier time containing his response to her. His mind and his body had never been at odds like this. Why was he having visions of her taking off his clothes, the two of them rolling naked across tangled sheets? She was at best a liar. And a thief.

Yet he'd discerned a hint of vulnerability he

couldn't banish. Perhaps deceit wasn't a normal part of her life.

While he knew little of the hormonal changes due to pregnancy, he wasn't completely ignorant. Pregnant women ate pickles and yearned for fresh strawberries; they didn't steal motorcycles. She couldn't be the innocent she wanted him to believe.

In court, she hadn't been as relaxed as she'd pretended. When the judge had agreed not to send her to jail, relief had washed across her tensed features. Although he suspected she wasn't pleased to find herself in his custody, she hadn't protested. She might not be a career criminal, but he'd bet everything he owned she was hiding something.

But what? There was nothing suspicious in her file. She'd left him with only one lead and he couldn't afford not to follow up.

He started the car. "I think we should talk to your grandmother."

Her fingers tightened around her purse, but her demeanor remained calm. She met his gaze with a curious hint of amusement. "Why?"

He admired her courage in the face of his resolve, but he had every intention of finding answers. If she wouldn't reply to his questions, then perhaps her family would. Sensing she didn't want him to meet her grandmother, he kept his tone reasonable, wondering how she'd avoid agreeing to his suggestion. Summer had many weapons in her arsenal and she was good at employing them all. He didn't know if she'd use sex, tears or an argument, and that intrigued him.

"You told the court your grandmother gave you a

hot bike. Don't you think you should talk with her about it?''

"Turn down Parson onto Fourth. She's at the Jarrod Home on Sunberry.''

Surprise left him speechless. He hadn't thought she'd so easily give in to his request. Summer's impetuous audacity amazed him. She was as unpredictable as an August rainstorm and twice as arousing. What was she up to?

She seemed almost too eager to bring him to her grandmother in Garden Grove and he couldn't understand why. Perhaps lack of sleep was causing his uncharacteristic inability to solve the mystery engulfing her. If she had something to hide, and she must, with all her evasive maneuvers, why would she want him near the one person who could prove her deceit?

Not for one moment did he believe she'd moved into his home so he could bond with his children. Nor did he think she was out to catch a husband. He'd dated too many woman who sized up his house and calculated his net worth not to recognize someone who wasn't motivated by greed.

So why was she bearing his children? What did she want from him? Why did she show up when he was just getting the business back on its feet? The short drive wasn't long enough to figure out the answers—not when he wasn't sure of the right questions.

The Jarrod Home looked more like a hotel than an assisted living center. Inside, the spacious foyer boasted a waterfall, and the pattering of the water echoed soothingly. Hallways of rich emerald carpet and flamingo pink tile led them past card and bingo rooms and a whirlpool and exercise area.

Seeing his interest, Summer commented, "Gran likes it here. She has her own apartment. Meals are served if she doesn't feel like cooking. Jarrod's arranges shopping and trips to the doctor, so though she can't drive anymore, she doesn't have to relinquish her freedom."

Her knowledge of the facility impressed him. Obviously, she cared about her grandmother.

They paused in the hall, waiting for a woman with a walker to turn toward the elevator. Potted palms in ceramic containers lined this corridor, giving the home the atmosphere of a luxury hotel.

A bleached-blond man in his late twenties and wearing white tennis shorts ambled toward them, a tennis racquet in his hand. "Hi, Summer. Almost didn't recognize you. Nice hair color."

"Thanks, Fred." Apparently, the man was accustomed to Summer's disguises. "Craig Banks, I'd like you to meet Fred Hardcastle."

Fred shook hands with Craig, but his gaze focused on Summer. "Gran's acting feisty."

Summer chuckled. "Did she beat you again?"

Fred winked. "Does her good when I let her win now and then. But that's not it."

"I give up. What's she done this time?"

Fred shook his head and grinned, showing off his white teeth against his tan as he passed by. "I'm not spoiling her surprise."

The cheerful man left Craig with an image of friendly concern. Not exactly the sterile and depressing picture he'd expected. If the rest of the staff were as upbeat and sympathetic as Fred, the residents were well cared for.

"How long has your grandmother lived here?"

"A few years. Fred's the athletic director. Gran says the women go to his clinics just to ogle his legs." They took an elevator up, and after a short walk down another hall, Summer stopped at a door decorated with a silver star, knocked and called out, "Gran."

"Coming, dear."

Craig angled himself to one side, positioning himself to observe Summer's face as the door opened. Instead of some secret signal, her eyes lit with joy, and she smiled with genuine warmth. She hugged the short and rounded woman, who appeared to be in her late seventies. Just as eccentric as her granddaughter, Gran wore jeans and a T-shirt, her thin hair dyed flaming red.

Summer leaned back from the embrace and examined the older woman. "I like your hair, Gran."

Her grandmother beamed and fluffed out a curl. "Really? I thought this look might be a little young for me."

"Naw. You don't look a day over fifty."

"What are you wearing, child?" She surveyed Summer's pin-striped suit. "Did someone die?"

"I had a business appointment," Summer explained.

Craig swallowed a grin as he wondered what her grandmother would have said about black leather. He suspected Gran would approve—especially if she had bought Summer that bike.

Gran peered around Summer. "Aren't you going to introduce me?"

Summer's lips turned up in an easy grin. "Gran, I'd like you to meet my friend, Craig Banks. He wants to ask about the motorcycle you bought me."

Gran fumbled for her pink-tinted John Lennon glasses and led them into a spotless den decorated in soft whites, aqua and peach. "Well, I don't know much about motorbikes. I paid two hundred dollars for it. Do you suppose that was too much?"

Craig took an overstuffed wing chair. Gran seated herself on the matching couch, pulled a Siamese cat into her lap and scratched it between the ears while Summer paced.

"Where did you buy the bike, ma'am?" Craig asked while Summer tossed her hair back from her face and gave him a warning look as if she expected he'd cross-examine the woman like a hostile witness.

"I always shop at the mall."

At Gran's curt, matter-of-fact reply, Craig restrained his astonishment. No mall he'd ever been to sold motorcycles. Had the old woman been conned? Or was he being set up? Summer had called Gran from his home. She'd had time to warn her that the bike was stolen. Was he too suspicious? Was Gran who she appeared—merely a dotty old lady with eccentric hair?

"Jarrod's bus provides daily trips to the mall," Summer reminded him.

"Did you get a title?" Craig asked, determined to learn the real story.

Gran looked bewildered. "I didn't buy any books. My eyes aren't what they used to be."

Craig choked on a chuckle.

Eyes twinkling Summer took a seat on the couch. "Gran, he means did you get a...receipt for the bike?"

Gran shook her head and, with a girlish gesture, twisted her finger in her red hair. "That's why I got a good deal. The salesman told me September is a special month for sales—like a flea market. Bought it—as is, where is." She beamed with pride at remembering the correct terminology. "Didn't it run good?"

There could be no doubting Summer's love for her grandmother as she patted Gran's hand. "The motor ran just fine." Summer turned to him. "Is there anything else you need?"

He felt like a heel, trying to trip up the grandmother to catch Summer in a lie. Yet she was hiding something; he sensed it by the challenging glint in her too-green eyes. He turned back to the elderly woman. "Just one more question, please. When did you buy the bike?"

Summer crossed her legs and her foot bounced nervously, the heel of her shoe slipping off one elegant foot, pink nail polish winking at him. He fought down a twinge of desire.

"Let me see. Fred brought me a chicken dinner that day. I think it was Friday. No, Friday is fish day." Gran scratched her neck. Her eyes widened. "Sorry. I can't remember. Is it important?"

Summer stood and leaned over to embrace her grandmother. "No. It's not important."

Craig had difficulty keeping his gaze off Summer's long, lean legs. She didn't seem to notice, but he thought her grandmother did, because behind Summer's back, she gave him the thumbs-up signal.

"Thanks for your help, Gran. We've got to go." Summer kissed the woman's cheek. "I'll be in touch."

As Craig drove home, Summer lay back against the headrest. Her face still looked tired, but the tension had eased from her shoulders.

"You seem especially close to your grandmother."

"I am."

She spoke reluctantly, and he wondered if his suspicions were running rampant. She'd told him precious little about her family, even less about her past. She hadn't mentioned friends, either. The way she avoided his questions told him not to trust her.

Wanting to do something normal to ground him in reality, Craig pulled over at an ice-cream stand along the beach. The sun had set and the first stars glittered in the night sky, adding to his strangely restless mood. Lack of sleep and the surprises of the day, not the woman beside him, had caused a tautness to hum through him.

From the moment she woke him this morning, the day had held a fast-forward quality, and he suddenly ached for the peace of a moonlit stroll on a beach with a pretty woman at his side.

"So you grew up with your grandmother?"

"Gran raised me. It wasn't easy for her, burying a son. She treated me like a daughter—a hellion, she called me."

He chuckled, picturing Summer as a mischievous ten-year-old. "Now you causing trouble—*that* I don't find hard to believe." He spotted a place where the cliffs broke. Moonlight illuminated a path down to the Pacific. "How about an ice-cream cone and a walk?"

"Sure. I need the calcium."

Ten minutes later, she was licking chocolate off her lips while he tried to think of something besides drawing her into his arms. Besides kissing her.

Other couples strolled along the shore. Several people walked their dogs. Someone rode a skateboard with a sail attached down the beach—typical Southern California, September craziness.

To avoid bumping her, Craig unclipped his cell phone from his belt and reattached it to his other side. Summer slipped off her heels. As they strolled side by side, he recalled the softness of her breasts pressing against him when she'd clung to him earlier. He recalled the feel of her in his arms, the scent of vanilla, the tender way she'd placed his hand over her womb, and he ached to—

Stop it. What the hell was wrong with him? The woman had secrets that might be vital to the welfare of his children. Instead of thinking about romance, he should be grilling her about her past.

"Where's the rest of your family?"

"Gran and her brother are the only family I have."

"And your parents?"

"My parents died in a car crash when I was ten. My grandparents were the only family I had left— except for Gran's useless younger brother, Bob."

"Useless?"

"Bob only came around when he needed money for liquor. He was famous for ranting about some missing stock that Gran said couldn't possibly exist."

"So you lived with your grandparents?"

"Yes. Two years after my parents' car accident, Grandfather died, leaving Gran to take care of me alone. Gran never once complained, scrubbing floors to earn the money to raise me. She'd come home and prepare my favorite foods, and at night, she'd sew doll clothes for my collection."

Summer stumbled over a rock. He reached out to prevent her from falling.

A rifle shot cracked the air.

Chapter Three

A bullet whizzed past the spot where Craig's head would have been if he hadn't bent to catch Summer. Closer to the water, a rock shattered. Additional bullets ricocheted into the ocean with hissing whines.

Summer's heart slammed her ribs. The initial firecracker pops of the shots choked the air and echoed along the cliffs. People on the beach screamed and shouted in panic. Had the shooter fanned the waterfront with a spray of ammunition? Or had she been the real target?

In the distance a dog barked, and car headlights on the highway above slowed to a stop.

He'd found her.

If Craig hadn't leaned forward, he might be dead. She'd put Craig in danger. The babies in danger. That shot had been meant for her.

Oh, God. What had she done?

"Come on." Craig grabbed her hand and yanked her toward the safety of the cliffs, out of the line of fire.

Shots zinged by, spattering dirt.

Hand in hand, they zigzagged, sprinting over the

rough terrain. Her breath came in rasps, stabbing her with guilt. Her eyes brimmed and she stumbled, would have fallen if not for Craig's steadying hand.

Within seconds, they'd reached the relative protection of the cliff's base. Above, the cliff's inky silhouette blacked out the stars. The shadows hid the sniper from view.

Craig tugged her in the direction of the ice-cream stand. "Let's work our way to my car."

"No!" She dug in her heels and resisted with every ounce of strength she had, almost toppling him.

"But—"

"Whoever fired those shots will expect us to return to your car. He'll pick us off along the way."

"Fine. We'll stay here until help arrives." He opened his cell phone. "I'll call the police."

"No." She grabbed the phone, her voice low, urgent and as forceful as she could make a whisper. "There's no time. We have to flee."

"What are you talking about?"

Despite the weariness tugging at her, her instinct to run was ingrained. She wasted several seconds trying to convince him that fleeing was their only option. "The sniper will work his way down from the cliffs before help arrives."

"He may not follow us."

His tone had a sharp deadliness she'd never heard before. She urged him farther away from the ice-cream stand, staying close to the cliff's base for protection.

Her skin broke into a sweat in the cool night air. "There's no time to explain. He's after me. He knows he didn't succeed. You can go. I've got to hide, then escape.'' She glanced up at the cliffs. ''He'll be hunting me, and I need to take cover.''

''What makes you think he's only after you?'' He uttered an inarticulate growl. ''It doesn't matter. I'm not leaving you alone.''

Grateful he'd stay with her and thankful he had the good sense not to waste precious time with more questions, she held tightly to his hand. The night had already thrown her one too many curves, and staying alive took priority over making explanations. Hugging the shadows of the cliff that separated them from the road above and shielded them from the sniper, they stumbled along the beach at the foot of the precipice.

From the direction of the ice-cream stand, flashlights shone in their direction. If the beams caught them, the sniper would have a clear shot.

Move faster.

Craig's husky tone encouraged her. ''We're almost there.''

There? She saved her breath and, with a last surge of adrenaline, lunged into the shadows of huge boulders that rose from the rocky beach. Ducking behind a car-size rock, she halted and gasped air into oxygen-starved lungs.

Craig, barely breathing hard, pointed to a dark spot about twelve feet above them. ''Can you climb up there?''

''If there are stairs.''

He ignored her sarcasm. ''I'll help you.''

Her hands shook, but she kept the fear from her voice. *How ridiculous.* It was a measure of her panic that they might be about to die and she was worried whether Craig thought her brave.

"Wait here. Let me check it out." He disappeared into the darkness. His clothing rustled. She heard a grunt. A few seconds later, he reappeared beside her. "I found a four-foot indentation that cuts the wind and a lip that'll hide us."

A police siren wailed. Lights advanced along the beach.

Gulping air, Summer forced herself to go on. "Lead the way."

In the end, she tossed her shoes up before attempting the climb. Craig found small ledges and smaller handholds in the cliff face and talked her up part of the way. Two feet short of the cave's floor, she couldn't reach the next handhold. Craig climbed around her, then hauled her up with the smooth ease of an Olympic athlete.

Just in time. The lights would reach them soon. Drawing back into the nook, she placed her shoes on feet that felt like ice cubes. Her teeth chattered, and Craig drew her into his arms, sharing his warmth and pressing her farther into the shadows.

When she shivered, he removed his jacket and placed it around her shoulders. She snuggled into the remaining warmth of his body heat, protesting in a murmur, "You'll freeze."

"Not with you in my arms," he whispered huskily.

He gathered her close, his hands on her shoulders, and tucked her head under his chin. He rubbed warmth into her back, courage into her spine. She told herself leaning against him was a normal reaction after almost being killed. With him protecting her, she felt out of danger. A perilous assumption. Whoever had shot at them had found her. Obviously, she hadn't done a good enough job of disappearing.

Because of her bungling, she'd put Craig and his children at risk. What would he do if she told him the truth? When she'd planned her escape, she hadn't considered she might endanger Craig Banks—or develop feelings for him. As he stood in the dark, defending and warming her with his body, she realized she owed him the truth. It was time to confess, take the consequences and hope the babies wouldn't suffer, too.

Despite the danger, she had to explain while she still could. Careful to keep her voice to just a murmur, she tugged on his arm. "Craig?"

"Yes?" He shifted so she could see the light beams searching the cliffs. They still had several minutes to converse in low tones before they risked being overheard by the searchers.

She leaned into him, wondering how much she should reveal. Craig shifted again, and her thoughts scattered. His hand cupped her chin, gently tugging her face toward him.

"Are you cold?"

"Yes. No. I'm not sure."

She sensed his grin. When they finally left this nook, they might die. Yet with him holding her close, her ear pressed to the reassuring beat of his heart, she felt safe.

He wrapped protective arms around her like a cozy wool blanket. Sharing the heat from his coat, she drank in the warmth of his nearness, relieved she didn't have to bear this by herself. He held her cradled against his chest as if she were precious and fragile glass. She'd been held before—but never like this.

A part of her hungered for his understanding while a more logical part accused her of doing the unforgivable. While necessity focused concern on their immediate survival, if they lived, she'd eventually have to answer his questions.

There was no way she could justify her deception.

Imminent danger combined with her hormonal imbalance must be altering her perception. She wrenched herself from his embrace. What had he done to her? A simple hug couldn't be that good, that warm, that comforting.

Having few experiences to compare with this one left her confused and attempting to gather her rioting emotions. She'd love to accuse him of taking advantage of the situation. But he hadn't taken anything she hadn't been willing to give.

Someone below let out a shout.

"Have they spotted us?" she whispered.

"I don't think so. Just hold still and the shadows should hide us."

She obeyed instantly. What kind of rapport was forming between Craig and her? Did fear escalate other emotions? She quailed at the possibility that she'd responded to him because of the babies growing inside her. Encircled by Craig's warmth, she stood in the dark, the scent of his mint-chocolate-chip ice cream lingering in her nostrils, his embrace taunting her with unnamed longing. And she had no clue to *his* thoughts, *his* feelings or *his* motivations.

It didn't matter. Right now, they needed to concentrate on staying alive.

She forced her attention to the events below. After what seemed like hours, the search party with flashlights left the beach, and Craig helped her down to the sand. Peering through the dark, she expected a shot to her back, agonizing pain between her shoulder blades. The wind picked up off the water, and the chilly humidity caused her to burrow deeper into Craig's coat. In just a thin shirt, he must be freezing. If not for her pregnancy, she would have insisted on returning his jacket.

"Are you up for a short walk?" His voice was as calm as if asking her to stroll in the park.

They couldn't return to his car. She opened her mouth to protest but closed it with a snap when he briskly led her in the opposite direction from which they'd come.

She hurried to keep up with his longer stride. "Where are we going?"

"Ahead of us, the beach widens." He tilted the cell phone in the moonlight and pressed numbers. "Let's hope Brad's at home."

"Whoever Brad is, tell him to bring a rope." At the thought of scaling the towering cliffs in the dark, she shuddered.

"Rock climbing shouldn't be necessary. Up ahead, there's a path between the cliffs that leads to the road."

Thirty minutes later, they flagged down Brad's car. Summer was grateful for the warmth as she slid into the back seat of the vehicle. Craig took the front seat beside his friend.

Brad grinned a greeting. "Where to?"

"Home."

"No." Summer leaned forward. "Take us some-where unexpected. Somewhere we can hide."

At her suggestion, Craig stiffened, but then he turned in his seat half-facing her and nodded. "We can pick up another car at my office. Then Brad can go home, okay?"

Brad's brows lifted, and he opened his mouth to speak.

His eyes resembling the darkest of rain clouds, Craig cut him off, his words sure and strong. "Don't ask. The lady owes *me* an explanation first."

AFTER A SOOTHING SHOWER at Craig's ski chalet in the Sierras, Summer, wrapped in a thick robe, sat be-fore a massive stone fireplace. She sipped hot choc-olate while across from her Craig lifted the stopper from a cut-glass decanter.

In a few weeks, Summer knew, the mountains would cast spectacular fall colors across the hills and valleys. Even this early, the mountain air had a chill. But the air around Craig was frigid.

"I'll leave in the morning," she told him softly. "If this cabin's in your name, I can't stay here long."

Craig's eyes narrowed at the implication. "Let me get this straight. If you stay, the sniper will find you?" The silence stretched out for several long minutes. He poured himself a bourbon, downed the liquor in one easy swallow, then poured another. He pinned her with a hard look, his eyes so dark they let in no light at all. "What makes you think that sniper was after you and not someone else on the beach?"

She remained silent a moment, trying to put her thoughts in order before answering. Where should she start? How could she make him understand what she'd done?

Craig scowled. "Since my life and my children are at risk, you'd best tell me who's after you."

"I don't know."

She shifted uneasily, wondering if she'd ever feel safe again. Would she be forced into hiding and lying for the rest of her life? Outside, the wind howled like a wild animal. Despite the cozy fire and the comfortable cabin, Summer shivered.

His lips twisted with disbelief. "You have no idea who's trying to kill you?"

"None. There have been other incidents. I was scared. I went to the police."

"They couldn't protect you?" He tightened his long fingers around the glass until the sharp edges had to be cutting into his palm. Judging from the muscle clenching and unclenching in his jaw, he was furious. Yet she knew by now he wouldn't hurt her.

Ah, how she wished she could tell him everything.

"I'm not even sure the police believed me. I had no proof." She twisted her mug in her hands and finally set it down before guilt, warring with anger and fear, caused her to spill the steaming chocolate. "I didn't want to prove I was right by providing them with my corpse."

She didn't want to tell him what she'd done next. Picking up her napkin, she wadded the paper into a ball, then slowly shredded it. She *had* to tell him. Even if it ruined their tentative truce. The comforting embrace they'd shared on the beach made admitting her deception so much more difficult. Not just because she'd tried so hard only to have everything blow up in her face, but because, she grudgingly admitted to herself, she was starting to care about him.

Without the lies to protect her, she'd have to survive his wrath—and hope that his love for the children outweighed his anger at her. Tossing aside the shredded napkin, she crossed her arms and rubbed the goose bumps on her arms. Putting off the worst revelation a moment longer, she licked her stiff, dry lips.

"I've lied to you. And Gran lied to you after I called her and told her what to say. You have to understand, I didn't think he'd find me." She dropped her head into her hands, despair invading her heart. Craig deserved better. Somehow she found the strength to raise her head and lock gazes with him. "This morning, I was in the park and a man on a motorcycle tried to kill me."

Believe me. Please.

"What did he look like?" he snapped, impatience clear in his voice.

She shrugged, trying not to let his obvious suspicion slice so deep. "He wore a helmet. The shield hid his features."

"Clever."

His eyes glittered, and she couldn't tell if he'd referred to her or her attacker, but either way his comment was no compliment. Nothing he could say would make the torment ripping her apart any worse. Soon he'd comprehend she'd done the unforgivable. His bloodless tone made her shudder. What would he do to her when he learned what she had to tell him? Only knowing this was the same man who'd taken such good care of her on the beach made it possible to go on.

She shoved to her feet. "After I got away from the motorcyclist, I found a police officer. When we returned, my assailant had vanished. I couldn't return to my apartment or use my car. I told the cop the bike was mine."

"Why?"

"I needed to disappear. Fast." She gave a choked, desperate laugh and paced. Anything was better than guessing what he was thinking. "I was so shaken, I could barely remember I'd once been taught how to ride a bike. The black leather clothes I found in the saddlebags seemed like a gift."

When he said nothing, she risked a glance at him. He raised an eyebrow, his expression saying better than any comeback what he thought of her story. But she needed him to believe her.

"That's when I came to you," she continued, ashamed he thought her capable of callously taking advantage of him when she'd wanted to give him something good and pure. She ached to reach out and soothe the worry lines on his face with the tips of her fingers, yearned to take him into her arms. Instead, she said simply, "I had nowhere else to go."

His eyes darkened with skepticism. "Where did the duffel bag come from?"

If there was a way to brace herself for his wrath, she had yet to find it. She trembled inside, knowing he would soon slice to the heart of the matter. "I'd stashed the duffel in a locker at the bus station."

"You were prepared for an attack?" Incredulity laced his tone.

She took a deep breath, released the air out in a hiss, raised her chin and finally spoke with a forcefulness she was far from feeling. "I've been threatened before. This is the second time I've had to...disappear."

His face creased with a frown, the tiny lines around his troubled eyes deepening. "I don't understand."

"I never intended to put your children at risk," she hesitantly began.

As comprehension dawned before she had a chance to spell out the rest, Craig hurled his half-empty bourbon glass into the fireplace. The glass shattered into a million shards. Flames roared up as if to ridicule her.

Feeling as though he'd slapped her, she flinched at the smoldering anger beneath the controlled exterior. His nostrils flared, the only visible concession to his rage.

Craig turned on her, his fists raised, his shoulders rigid, a muscle pulsing in his jaw. "You agreed to become a surrogate mother so you could vanish, didn't you? You used me and my unborn children to disappear."

She winced at his accusation, felt the blood draining from her face. What she wouldn't give to take back her decision. He had every right to be furious with her. Sorrow and guilt racked her, but she stiffened and faced him. "I never thought—"

"That's right—you didn't think. You didn't think you were risking the lives of my children." He advanced.

She retreated until she backed against the wall, the robe slipping down one shoulder. Trapping her, he leaned forward, flattening his palms on both sides of her head.

Her lungs refused to draw in a breath. "I didn't think he'd find me. It was the perfect plan. I left my job. I didn't tell anyone where I was going. I started a new life."

"How can you act as if you're blameless?"

She shivered at the chill in his tone, the dark scowl on his lips, the icy fury in his eyes. With a touch as delicate as an artist's, he slid his long fingers over her neck to the curve of her shoulder.

"Don't—"

"Don't what? Don't let your wide, innocent eyes distract me from the truth? Don't listen to the words from your lying lips?" He yanked the robe back over her shoulder, his gaze dropping briefly to the valley between her trembling breasts. "If you catch cold, my children might suffer."

She snatched the material and held the edges together like a shield. "I hoped some good could come from this. I hoped to give you what you wanted— your children."

Fierce eyes, burning coal gray and reflecting sparks of firelight, seared her. His hands clenched and unclenched. "Instead, you risked their lives before they've even been born."

"I thought I was safe," she repeated, choking on the words, knowing he didn't believe her and wondering bitterly why he should.

"How long did it take him to find you after you disappeared the first time?"

"Six weeks." She told herself she deserved whatever he said. But she shook inside. That something could turn so bad when she'd been so full of good intentions filled her with intolerable sadness.

He gripped her shoulders, his hold almost painful as he pinned her to the wall. "Today, he found you within hours. He must have followed you."

"I was careful."

He pierced her with a you-can't-be-that-naïve scowl, and she couldn't blame him. By going to him for help, she'd put his life at risk along with her own. If whoever was after her succeeded, the babies would die with her. He had every right to be furious. Still, it hurt, and she shriveled a little at his contemptuous expression.

She'd been so careful after she'd left her job and moved. She hadn't contacted her friends. She'd even changed her hair color. So how had he found her?

Craig grabbed her upper arm none too gently and shoved her onto the sofa. He sat on the coffee table in front of her, his elbows planted on his knees, his face inches from hers. "You must have some idea who's after you."

She swallowed the lump in her throat and raised her chin to look him in the eyes. "If I did, I wouldn't have come to you. I'd have tracked him down."

Her response seemed to have no effect on him, but then he was good at concealing his thoughts. Only his eyes revealed the bitterness, and though he had not said what he planned to do, she had a feeling in her gut that he would make her pay.

"You told me your parents are dead," he half said, half asked.

"Yes." His seemingly abrupt change in questioning had her stomach doing flip-flops, but she stuck to the truth where she could.

"The file said you've never been married."

"Yes."

"Don't yes me. You've been damn secretive about your past. I want details. Surely you've been involved in relationships. You haven't lived your life as a hermit. You've known neighbors, co-workers, bosses and friends. Were the partings bitter or amicable? Where do your ex-boyfriends live?"

The physicians at the clinic had asked detailed questions about her medical history and background before agreeing to accept her as a surrogate, but those files were sealed to him. He only knew what his attorneys knew, and that information she'd concocted in order to hide from the stalker.

She supposed he had every right to ask such personal questions; still, she resented his intrusion into her private affairs. "Kendrick and I broke up two years ago. Our parting wasn't especially bitter. We never lived together."

She sensed him mentally reviewing her file before cracking out his next question like a drill sergeant. "What about your job? A flight attendant meets all kinds of people. Were you dating?"

Tell him. She twisted her hands on her thighs. "I wasn't a flight attendant."

He rubbed his chin in exasperation, but his gaze never left hers. "Were you an undercover cop? Don't tell me you work for the CIA."

"Nothing so hazardous. I'm a legal secretary."

"Where?"

She kept twisting her fingers, noted her outward sign of nervousness but couldn't stop fidgeting. "My first job was with Harry Pibbs's law office, a small firm in the valley."

"And your second job?"

She should never have worked as a legal secretary again, but she'd hated to give up all contact with the law. The deciding factor had been money. No other job that she was offered paid as well as a legal secretary. When Gran's monthly bill at the nursing home had been overdue, she couldn't let them evict her.

At Gran's age, changes didn't come easy. Not that Gran complained. When Summer first brought her to Jarrod's, Gran's confusion and fear slowly turned to pleasure at her surroundings. Summer had vowed not to move Gran again. After all Gran had done for her, it was now time for Summer to return the love.

But she refused to make excuses to Craig. "I worked at Dean, Atherson, and Jackson."

As she named his attorneys' office as her last place of employment, he flinched as if hit by a bullet. His voice flayed her with scorn. "You set me up from the start."

"While I worked as a legal secretary, I saw your letter asking the firm to find a surrogate, applied for the position through the fertility clinic and concocted a background to match your requirements."

Please let him understand.

"It was my chance to disappear. Leave my job. Vanish. You have to believe I didn't think he'd find me."

Craig's threatening stare held her in an iron-tight lock. "As a legal secretary, what kind of cases did you work on?"

"Nothing criminal." She knew where his questions were leading since she'd asked herself the same things a hundred times. Always she came up with zip.

She couldn't think of a reason anyone would want her dead. "Mostly divorces. Sometimes I helped with the probate of an estate."

He stood and paced like a magnificent animal in a cage, the tension in his shoulders holding him rigid. "We need to talk to my attorney. I want to go through their files."

"You can't do that. It violates attorney-client privilege."

His dark face grew taut and derisive. "Then what are *you* suggesting?"

Despair settled over her like a veil at the thought she'd lost all chance to win his respect without ever really knowing him. He didn't seem to realize she wasn't just a body to carry his children, but a person with hopes and dreams and goals. She'd put law school on hold while she hid from the stalker, but she fully intended to graduate one day. She'd worked too hard and too long to give up.

Despite the lies she'd been forced to tell to survive, she had nothing to be ashamed of. She hadn't hurt anyone. Pride kept her head high. She refused to let him see her unhappiness.

"Just find me a place to hide somewhere close by so I can look after Gran. You needn't visit or call me. After the babies are born, our deal will be finished. I'll no longer be your concern."

"Lady, I'm not sure I believe a word you've told me. The court placed you in my custody, and I'm not letting you out of my sight. Besides, I still don't understand why we can't go home."

"The stalker followed your car to the beach and probably has had your license tag traced. So he knows your name. And with a name, courthouse documentation will reveal every piece of property owned in this county.''

He shook his head. "My car is a company vehicle. There's no way it can be traced to me. So we can still go back to my house.''

Summer swallowed a groan. Although it had been prudent not to return to his car, there had been no need to drive all the way to the mountains. She felt like the child who'd called wolf without reason, yet how could she have anticipated the car wasn't registered in his name? They'd fled to the ski chalet when they could have simply called a cab and gone back to his home.

"I'm sorry.''

Beneath the calm, she sensed squelched fury, but he spoke evenly. "I'd rather take extra precautions and be safe than risk my children's lives. Under the circumstances, you did the right thing." He paused, anger repressed beneath a polished civility. "Have you considered you're being followed when you visit your grandmother?''

"I'm extremely careful. I always approach and leave from different directions. Sometimes I walk, other times I take a taxi or bus. And I wear disguises.''

"You can't be sure he's not picking up your trail there.''

"I'm not sure of anything. But the stalking started before Gran moved into Jarrod's.''

He leaned forward, his expression tense. "Why can't we go to the police?''

"Without evidence, they can't do anything. I tried

once before, and not only wouldn't the cops help, as I left the police station, I was threatened."

"How?"

She shuddered, wondering if she'd ever again feel safe. "I found a typed note on my car windshield."

His eyes flashed a combination of frustration, curiosity and anger. "What did the note say?"

She didn't want to tell him. The threat sounded so melodramatic, and once again she hadn't gotten a peek at her assailant. As the icy determination in Craig's stormy eyes raked her, she licked her bottom lip nervously.

A tremor caressed her spine as she repeated the eerie words that haunted her nightmares. "The note was a threat. It said, 'Don't come back. I'll be watching.' It was signed, 'The Sentry.'"

"What happened to the note?"

"I was so frightened...I tore it into pieces." And she'd thrown it away, thrown away her only piece of hard evidence. Afterward, she wondered if she'd been hasty. Perhaps the police could have taken prints off the paper.

Craig loomed over her like a lion about to pounce on his prey, his expression guarded. "Is there anything else you haven't told me?"

Chapter Four

As Craig skimmed the leaves from his backyard pool the following afternoon, Summer reclined in a lounge chair, trying to hide the dark circles beneath her eyes with sunglasses. Although he'd asked her to write up a list of suspects, he could no more press her for answers now than he could last night at the ski chalet after she'd evaded his question.

Damn it. He tightened his fingers on the skimmer's pole. He'd banked most of the anger heating his veins after realizing she hadn't deliberately endangered his children. Even so, he sensed her holding back secrets and he wanted to shake more information out of her. What could she still be hiding? Last night, Summer had balked at answering that question. Instead, hesitating as though the breath she took would be her last, she'd lowered her gaze to the floor, her long lashes veiling her eyes.

Finally, she'd shaken her head, a lock from the blond wig falling over her pain-filled expression. He still didn't know her natural hair color. Today, her wig was a tawny maple with burnished sandy highlights. Not even her sunglasses hid the look of an-

guish on her face, although whether her feelings were
a result of the peril she'd put his children in, or for
herself, he couldn't tell.

She hunched over a memo pad, nibbling the eraser
between her straight white teeth, her full lips pursed.
Every once in a while, she scribbled something, often
scratching it out.

While he skimmed the pool's surface of windblown
grass, water bugs and oak leaves, he vowed to remain
indifferent to her and approach their problems in a
businesslike manner. He allowed himself to admire
her legs. Lots of women had long, lean legs tanned
to a golden hue. So what?

That's it. Reduce her to impersonal body parts,
each quite lovely. Get over her sensual, slender fingers with pink-tipped nails. Ignore the tiny frown
marring her lush mouth. Pretend it didn't matter that
she seemed to care about his babies as much as he
did.

With a groan of disgust, she threw down the pad
and drew her knees to her chest. "This is futile. I
have no idea who is after me."

Forcing his gaze from her legs, he dumped the
leaves into a pile, put down the skimmer and picked
up a brush. Squatting, he scrubbed the tiles, meticulously working around the pool's rim. "Most stalkers
are ex-boyfriends or ex-husbands."

"Kendrick Yarlboro might have some bizarre
ideas, but..."

At her words he dropped the scrub brush into the
water. "What kind of bizarre ideas?"

Her mouth curved faintly. "Kendrick believes horror movies shouldn't just show the blood and gore.

He wants the audience to experience the terror. According to him, films today depend upon special effects instead of psychological terror. He thinks movies should tap into the human psyche's fears.''

Wonderful. That this memory of the man could make her grin caused some concern. Kendrick had to be their prime suspect. Craig held his suspicions to himself, retrieved the floating scrub brush and maintained his unemotional tone. "What's Kendrick do for a living?"

"He's a successful horror writer, but he wants to produce movies."

How could she tell him that so calmly? She'd dated someone who created terror as easily as Craig imported chopsticks. Her former boyfriend probably knew more about stalking than the police. Summer must have good reasons to believe Kendrick innocent. She was an intelligent woman, one who'd had the foresight to store clothing, disguises and cash at the bus station. On the beach, she'd remained unruffled under gunfire. Yet any woman could be brilliant—except when it came to judging men.

He advanced to the tile by the shallow end of the pool. "Where does he live?"

"L.A. Where else?"

Her flippant answer peeled away a layer of his composure, and he snapped at her in a tone harsher than he intended. "So he has the imagination to stalk you. He lives close enough to have the opportunity. But you don't think he's behind your problems?"

"He doesn't have a motive," she flung back without an instant's hesitation. "He isn't passionate enough about me to be a stalker."

Her statement almost had him dropping the scrub brush again. How could any man not be passionate about Summer? When she wasn't making him furious, when he wasn't protecting her and the babies, he was thinking about her pink nails raking his back, her long legs wrapped around his waist, the softness of her lips during a passionate kiss. "Why?"

"All Kendrick's passion goes into his work. He hadn't much time or feeling left over for me."

She spoke in a clipped tone, and he sensed the effort it cost to tell him—almost as though she believed there was something wrong with her if Kendrick hadn't felt passionate about her. Craig knew better. Kendrick was even weirder than she realized.

"Was it your idea to end the relationship?"

"It was mutual. We just drifted apart. There were no acrimonious feelings. He still calls occasionally, but I've been out of touch for weeks now."

He stopped scrubbing, looked up and wished he could see her eyes without the sunglasses. "Why does he keep calling?"

Summer's brows drew together. "We liked each other. We didn't think our friendship had to end just because we're no longer together."

He supposed not. Craig tried to accept what she'd told him objectively but found he couldn't. A horror writer had to have a twisted mind. Perhaps Kendrick had taken Summer for granted until they'd split up. Maybe he hadn't realized how much he'd wanted Summer until she'd left. Could his passion have turned from writing stories to stalking a woman in the hope of frightening her into coming back to him? Or was Craig imagining this scenario because he wanted to identify the stalker quickly and move her out of his home before he did something stupid, like kiss her?

"Who else is on your list?"

"No one."

"All that scribbling and you couldn't come up with another name?"

She inhaled and let out her breath in an audible sigh. "I've been trying desperately to think of some suspects. It hasn't been easy. Between trying to hide and work, I've had to concentrate on survival. I've lived in Santa Del Ray or Garden Grove my entire life, but the possibilities are barely limited. Whoever is doing this started before I worked for your attorney's firm and before I moved Gran into the nursing home. I'm discounting everyone I met at the new job or at the nursing home."

That made sense. The stalker could be anyone—a former teacher or neighbor or friend. There was always the possibility a complete stranger had become fascinated with her as she paid for her groceries. Yet they had to go with the odds that favored the stalker being someone she knew.

"What about that guy at the nursing home, Fred? He certainly has the opportunity."

"What reason would he have to stalk me? He sees me all the time. Besides, he's got a girlfriend."

"All right. Why don't you tell me about your first job."

"There's not much to tell. It was a one-attorney office. I was one of three legal secretaries, and another woman came in twice a week to balance the books and to pay the bills."

"And your boss?"

"Harry Pibbs is a happily married man with two teenage daughters. He practices divorce and estate law."

Harry had been her mentor. He'd encouraged her to finish college and pursue a career in law. He'd been almost like a second father to her. Although he was still in good enough shape to ride a motorcycle, she found the idea so abhorrent she might as well try to picture Santa Claus as a stalker.

"Did he ever make a pass at you?"

She winced and drew her knees tighter to her chest. "Do you think I would have worked there for three years if he had? Besides, he's been a friend of the family for years. He settled the estate for Gran after my parents were killed."

"All right, let's put Harry toward the bottom of your list. What about clients? Some of the estates must have involved large amounts of money."

"I only typed the documents."

He moved toward the pool's deep end but turned to keep her in view. "Some of the divorces must have been bitter. Couples fighting over assets, that sort of thing."

She shrugged. "So what?"

"Did you ever hear clients mention valuables they didn't want their spouses to know about?"

"All the time."

Finished scrubbing, he tossed the brush in a bucket. "Did any of these add up to significant amounts of money?"

She shook her head. Then suddenly, she jerked her chin up. There had been a case like that. A bitter dispute over child custody with both parents wanting control over the kid's trust fund. "What could this have to do with me?"

"I'm not sure." He stooped to check the chlorine level. "Put the client on your list along with your boss. We need to come up with some names no matter how unlikely."

She scribbled on the memo pad. "Then what?"

"Then we find out if they have an alibi while we were being shot at."

SUMMER AND CRAIG waited for the elevator at Jarrod's. Although annoyed that Craig insisted on accompanying her, she was grateful he'd agreed to visit Gran.

"Thanks for bringing me."

Mesmerized by the sudden warmth in his eyes, she savored the feeling of closeness. Today was the first time he'd treated her with anything but indifference since the night she'd told him about the stalker. He'd been so furious then, she'd been afraid he wouldn't govern his anger, and what shreds of control she'd had left began to crumble. When he'd focused the harsh power of his dark eyes on her, she'd realized his appearance of a businessman was a thin veneer.

After her heart had stopped pounding, she'd figured out that beneath Craig's eminently sensible surface, he hid a frothing vitality, a furious tension and sizzling heat. Yet while the fire in his eyes had blazed with fury, and though he might hate her for putting the lives of his children in jeopardy, she was certain he had wanted to take her to bed.

No matter how much she enraged him, she'd felt

his compelling fascination with her. She'd sensed the powerful sentiments were almost beyond his capability to fight, and it had taken all her willpower to stand up to him when she should have been running away.

Looking at him now, the facade of a business executive wrapped securely around him once more, she saw the epitome of polish and sophistication. His gaze was tender, his actions patient and considerate. Yet, despite his tailored ivory shirt and pressed khaki slacks, she couldn't forget the man she'd glimpsed or the passions he kept hidden behind the cultured exterior.

He held the elevator door open for her politely, considerately, as if his anger had never been, and she wondered what was really going on in his head. Was he still furious with her for jeopardizing his children's safety but managing to hide his rage? Or had his anger dissipated with her explanation? Neither his tone nor his demeanor revealed any clues.

Even more importantly, she wondered why she cared. If he thought her a conniving bitch who'd deliberately risked his children's lives, nothing she said would change his opinion. She only wished she didn't mind. How could she prove that beneath the layers of lies she'd been forced to tell that she'd meant well? She had to try, yet with Craig's expression so stoic, she couldn't determine if she was making any headway.

Craig joined her inside the elevator and punched the button for Gran's floor. "This week is busy for me. While I can stay in touch by phone, fax and E-mail, I'll have to go into the office to sign a contract. I might not bring you back soon, so warn your grandmother.''

"Okay. I don't want her to worry."

They spoke to each other like polite colleagues. Was he attempting to make up for scaring her half to death the other night? Or was this a tactic to put her at ease so she'd confide in him? Or was he simply doing the best he could in an impossibly horrible situation?

The elevator stopped and the doors opened one floor below their destination. Summer automatically stepped aside to make room. She looked up to see Fred holding the door open with his tennis racquet while he escorted an elderly man by the elbow.

Fred pressed the button for the fifth floor, nodded at Craig but spoke to her, his gaze taking in her newest disguise with a grin. "Glad I caught you."

Summer's heart stuttered with worry. "Is Gran okay?"

"She's fine." Fred reached into the pocket of his white tennis shorts and retrieved a note. "Someone came by the old neighborhood looking for you this morning. I'd intended to give this message to your grandmother, but now I won't have to trouble her."

"Thanks, Fred." She reached for the note, hoping her hand wouldn't reveal her inner trembling. Who could be looking for her?

As if sensing the worry she couldn't shake, Craig draped his arm over her shoulder. She started to open the folded message when the elevator jerked and glided upward.

Fred stiffened, then lunged to keep a firm grip on the unsteady older man. "By the way—" Fred turned to Summer with a raised brow and a tanned grin showing off his white teeth "—you might want to remind your grandmother that her feet won't blister if she wears socks."

Summer rolled her eyes and grinned back. "I'll try to convince her, but you know how she is."

Fred laughed. "Don't I, though. She's always been stubborn."

The elevator deposited them on Gran's floor. Before the doors swished closed behind her and Craig, she'd opened the folded note and read it silently. "Have exciting news. How about dinner tonight? Give me a call." The note was signed "Kendrick," and he'd left his phone number.

Sensing Craig's burning curiosity, she handed him the note. He scanned the paper quickly before returning it. A sharp edge sliced his tone. "How did Kendrick know he could find you here?"

"He doesn't know I moved Gran to Jarrod's." She corrected his mistaken impression. "Fred picked up the message from Gran's house. His parents live a few doors away and have watched the house for me ever since I had to move out. Kendrick must have learned I'd moved and changed jobs. The only contact he has is Gran's house. He knows I'd never sell the property."

Her parents' house, the home she grew up in, had too many memories for her to consider giving up the property. The attic had been her favorite place to play. When she thought really hard, she sometimes caught the scent of her mother's perfume in the old clothes Summer used to play dress-up. The things were in storage now, the house leased, but she still dreamed of someday going home to live. But first, she had to figure out who was stalking her.

Craig's frown deepened until his forehead furrowed. "How often does Kendrick invite you to dinner?"

"Every few months. Why?" She stuffed the note into her purse and folded her arms over her chest. She didn't like Craig's personal questions about her past relationships, but under the circumstances, she allowed him more leeway than she would have another man.

His tone rose in conjecture. "You don't think his timing odd?"

They'd stopped beside Gran's door. Summer didn't knock, preferring to finish this conversation in private. Glancing into Craig's face, she noted how intently he watched her. Nervously, she licked her bottom lip. "What are you implying?"

"I'm not sure. In the past two days, you've been attacked in the park and shot at. You might run back to an old boyfriend for protection after such scares."

"Kendrick isn't trying to scare me into running back to him," she said emphatically, hoping he wouldn't want more explanations. She should have known better. Craig could be relentless when he wanted answers. She only wished the explanations she wanted to keep to herself didn't cause her so much pain to admit.

He arched an eloquent brow.

She raised her chin and spoke as if she didn't care. "I doubt Kendrick wants me back."

"Then he's a fool," Craig mumbled under his breath.

Odd how his words muted the sting of past failure. Even better, was it possible Craig cared for her more than he'd admitted?

Before she could question him, Gran opened the door, and Summer realized their words must have been louder than she'd thought. As they said hello, Summer told herself Craig couldn't possibly have feelings for her. She figured Craig meant he thought Kendrick a fool not to want her in bed.

All thoughts of Craig's meaning flew from her mind as Gran limped to the sofa.

Summer sucked in a gasp and hurried to her side. "What happened?"

"A little accident."

"I can see that. I'll bet fifty dollars you haven't had a doctor look at your foot."

Gran flushed guiltily. "It's my ankle. I just twisted it a bit during tennis."

"Fred said you were fine." Summer took Gran's elbow. "Come on. Lean on me."

Craig slipped an arm around Gran's waist and half carried her across the room. Between them, they soon had her seated on the sofa with her foot propped on a pillow. The cat leaped into her lap, circled and settled.

Gran leaned back with a groan. "Fred would have insisted on an X ray. The way that kid fusses over me, you'd think I was his own grandmother."

"You fed him enough cookies to *be* his grandmother." Summer shook her head. "Besides, Fred wouldn't have his job here if it wasn't for you. I'm glad he looks after you when I can't be here." With Gran's injury, she felt especially guilty about not giving her grandmother her phone number. Even Summer's infrequent visits could endanger Gran, too. Damn, what a mess! "You shouldn't have hidden the injury from Fred."

"Actually, the pain was just a twinge this morning. The swelling is worse now."

Craig walked into the kitchen and returned moments later with ice cubes in a plastic bag. He wrapped the bag in a hand towel and placed the ice gently on the swollen ankle. "Do you have aspirin?"

Gran leaned her head back and closed her eyes. "Ah, that feels better, thank you. Check the medicine cabinet over the bathroom sink."

"I'll be right back."

As soon as Craig disappeared, Gran's eyes popped open. Then she winked and gave Summer an impish smile. "You found a good man this time. Don't let him get away."

Gulp.

"Our relationship is strictly business. That's what I came to tell you."

Thankfully, before Gran could argue, Craig returned with a glass of water and a bottle of aspirin. "Summer may not be able to visit for a few days."

Gran reached for her hand and squeezed. "Sugar, he found you again?"

With Gran's injury, their original plan had to change, and she wished Craig hadn't revealed the stalker had found her. "Don't worry. I'm staying here until you're up and about."

"Absolutely not. I'll be fine." Gran shooed her away. "You go with your young man and let him protect you. Disappear as long as you have to. I understand."

Tears clogged Summer's throat. In spite of Gran's bravado, she heard a catch of fear in her voice. Until recently, her grandmother had always seemed so young and vital. She was both mother and father, the only relative Summer had except for the great-uncle she'd prefer to forget.

Gran had been there when Summer needed her. Now when it was her turn to repay the love, she couldn't deny Gran the care and attention she needed. "Gran, I'm not leaving you."

Craig took a chair opposite the sofa, rested his elbows on his knees. "How about a compromise? I'll pay a nurse for a few days to help until you're on your feet again. Summer will stay with me."

Gran gave Craig's plan an A-OK signal. Summer still hated the idea of leaving her grandmother alone. Since moving Gran again hadn't been an option—not with the waiting list for facilities as nice as this one—Summer's visits here had been the one part of her life she'd refused to change.

Sensing her agreement, Craig picked up the phone book, found the appropriate section and handed the phone to Gran.

Gran spoke quickly, then set down the receiver. "The agency promised to send someone right away."

Craig's offer was a generous solution. Although it was more to protect the babies than out of any particular kindness to Summer or Gran, gratitude filled her. "Thank you. When I'm working again, I'll repay you."

He simply nodded, and she thought she caught a

warm gleam in his eyes, a heated look implying he preferred another kind of payment. But after the cool way he'd been treating her, she must have been mistaken.

Summer waited until Gran swallowed the aspirin and set down her water glass before speaking. "Has anyone asked about me?"

Gran's fingers paused in scratching her cat between his ears. "No. And if they did, I'd never mention your name."

Craig stepped to the window and peered out. "It's important that you don't tell anyone where to find Summer."

"I won't slip up." Gran rolled her eyes at the ceiling. "Besides, she hasn't even told *me* where she's staying."

A knock on the door interrupted their conversation. "Are you expecting company?" Summer asked.

"Only if he's tall, rich and male," Gran quipped.

Summer stepped to the door and peered through the peephole. "It's Uncle Bob. What should I do?"

Gran pulled a pillow over her face. "Tell him I'm broke."

Craig frowned as Summer rubbed her brow. He joined her by the door. "Who is Uncle Bob?"

"Gran's younger brother. The one I told you about." She reached for the knob, wondering what she had done to bring so much bad luck at one time. She didn't like to be unkind, but right now they had more problems than they could handle. Experience had taught her that Uncle Bob would be difficult to get rid of if she let him inside. Knowing she had no real choice, she steeled herself for the inevitable confrontation, wondering what Craig would think of her only other family member. Craig was generous enough to pay for a nurse for Gran, but no doubt Uncle Bob was here to try to mooch off them.

Craig's hand closed over hers. "Don't open the door."

"He's three sheets to the wind. If I don't let him in, he'll start yelling at the top of his lungs." Summer shuddered and fought down embarrassment. "Someone will hear him and call security, who'll notify the police. It's better to get rid of him more quietly."

Gran groaned. "Tell the old bastard I died."

"Not a chance." Summer shook off Craig's hand and yanked open the door, uncaring if Bob Carlson heard her last statement. "He'd hang around, hoping to collect your last dime."

As usual, Uncle Bob looked successful. His distinguished gray hair and pressed suit belied his alcoholism. Gran's brother had been one of those surprise babies, arriving into the world almost twenty years after Gran. Now in his mid-fifties and in surprisingly good physical shape, he strode forward, his sharp eyes darting back and forth. As he stomped past her into the apartment, she caught a whiff of sour wine and stale cigarette smoke beneath the overpowering scent of peppermint.

Blocking the older man's progress, Craig advanced. With his legs spread, his feet planted in the carpet and his arms crossed over his chest, he cut a classic picture of intimidation. Uncle Bob didn't notice.

He shifted sideways. "Got anything to wet my parched throat?"

Gran lifted up her glass. "Here's some water."

Bob grimaced. "How about something with a bite to it?"

"You know Gran doesn't drink," Summer lied, wishing she and Gran could have been spared the annoyance of Bob's visit. Every family had one bad apple. Unfortunately, Bob was one of those individuals who tended to show up when he'd had too much to drink. She was tempted to give him what he sought, but she resisted. "Why are you here?"

Bob's eyes narrowed to tight, disapproving slits. "Same as you, missy. Paying my respects to family." He opened the refrigerator, then explored a few kitchen cabinets as if he owned the place. "If you cared about me, you'd offer me a drink."

"How about ten bucks?" Craig reached into his back pocket and pulled out his wallet.

Gran gasped.

Summer sighed as she fought down embarrassment. "Once you pay him, he'll expect constant handouts."

"This is a one-time offer." Craig slid a ten-dollar bill out and offered it to Bob.

Gran's brother licked his dry lips. With a shaking hand swollen with arthritis, he reached for the cash. "I wouldn't need this if she'd just give me the stock certificates."

Craig frowned. "What stock?"

Gran groaned. "It's a figment of his drunken imagination. If my son had owned stock, I would have cashed in the certificates long ago instead of spending years cleaning floors on my knees. And Summer wouldn't have had to work her way through law school."

"I didn't dream it up," Bob insisted, but he was clearly more interested in the current offering than the old discussion.

"I called Harry at the beginning of the semester," Summer admitted, "and asked him about the stock."

Gran's head jerked in surprise. "You did?"

"We were so short of money and I was hoping... But Harry said there had never been any stock in my parents' estate."

Bob paid no attention to the conversation. He staggered toward the money in Craig's hand.

Craig jerked back the bill—just out of reach. His tone was low, dangerously soft. "You aren't coming back, are you, Bob?"

Bob eyed him craftily. "For another ten in bus fare, I've got some people to see."

Craig folded the bill and placed the money in his shirt pocket, leaving a tempting corner hanging out. Bob's eyes focused uncertainly on the pocket. Silence filled the room.

Bob gave in first. "Well, I guess I could walk across town."

"You do that." Craig reached for the bill and stepped to the door. Bob followed like a puppy offered a bone. After Bob left, Craig snapped the lock. "Call security and tell them not to admit him again."

Summer released a pent-up breath. "We already have."

"He's sneaky," Gran added. "His usual modus operandi is to slip into the building while he flirts with one of the woman residents, holds open a door for her or helps carry a package."

The bell rang again and Craig opened the door to

admit the nurse sent by the agency. After Summer assured herself the woman would take good care of Gran, she and Craig strolled to the parking lot.

"Has your uncle Bob ever been in trouble with the law?"

"I don't know." Summer donned a pair of sunglasses, unsure if she was protecting herself from the bright sunlight or Craig's perceptive gaze. Resentful, she wondered if every male she'd ever known between the age of twelve and sixty had to come under scrutiny.

Before leaving the building, she scanned the parking lot for anyone who appeared to be waiting. No one seemed to be lurking. While the stalker may not have traced her to Craig's house, now that she was out, he could zero in on her again. Although she was careful to use various disguises when she called on Gran, she was always fearful the stalker could track her after her visit.

The California sun beat down, surprisingly strong for a fall day. But no one except a couple exiting a minivan was venturing out in the heat, and they seemed more interested in making a beeline for the air-conditioned building than in Summer's departure.

For a moment, her head spun with dizziness. She clutched Craig's hand to steady herself.

"What's wrong?" Concern radiated from his voice. He grasped her elbow with one hand and leaned her against his side.

"I'm just a little light-headed." Knowing Craig might forbid her to see Gran, Summer didn't mention her fear of the stalker following.

"We should get you to a doctor."

"That's not necessary. Going from the air-conditioning to the heat outside must have affected me. My hormones are changing as quickly as this weather."

He opened the car door for her and she slid inside, grateful when he didn't release his grip until she'd collapsed onto the seat. As soon as he started the engine, the cool air settled her, and she realized he was glancing over at her every other second with concern.

"I'm okay. I've read that pregnant women often feel faint. Most of the time I feel normal. Sometimes I actually forget about the twins."

"I can't forget." He said the words with such a combination of tenderness, regret and expectancy that she suspected this pregnancy would be as hard on him as on her.

"Raising children is a big step." She teased him gently, surreptitiously looking over her shoulder to make sure no one was following them. "You only have about eight more months to get ready."

He grimaced, and she realized she'd made a mistake to remind him how long they would be together, how long he had to protect her to keep his children safe. The air hummed with sudden tension. Conversation had suddenly become a high-wire act where she had to balance between survival and hunger for personal contact.

"How about we take a ride?" he asked.

"Where?"

He checked his watch and handed her his cell phone. "I want us to keep your dinner date with Kendrick."

Chapter Five

"Why are we stopping to pick up take-out food when Kendrick invited you to dinner?" Craig asked, trying to keep how odd he thought she was acting out of his voice.

Summer's low laugh tingled up his arm and warmed his blood. "I don't like bowling-alley food."

She tucked a bag steaming with the aroma of egg rolls, fried wonton and sautéed shrimp between them on the seat. As he inhaled the enticing aromas, his mouth watered. He must be hungrier than he'd realized.

However, since meeting Summer, all his senses seemed extraordinarily acute. As she shut her car door, the late-afternoon light shimmered off her latest wig, a rich chestnut cascade of curls that he longed to smooth away to explore the tantalizing mystery she'd hidden beneath.

Discovering what she really looked like was becoming a minor obsession. An expert chameleon, she changed hair color and style, eyes and facial features with wigs, contacts and makeup. The longer he knew her, the more sides of her he discovered.

Today, her luminous skin glowed with a surface translucence that deepened to a creamy complexion, a hint of blush on her cheeks. Yesterday, he would have sworn she'd had a tan. He'd never noticed a slight almond-shaped slant to her eyes before and wondered if he'd never looked closely enough or if she'd emphasized the appealing outline with makeup. Her irises alternately turned light brown to hazel to a deep green, the color enhanced by contacts or maybe the reddish highlights of her unruly chestnut hair.

Accustoming himself to the fascinating faces she showed to the world had become an engrossing part of his day, yet he was even more interested in knowing what drove her. One moment she was the caring granddaughter, the next a brazen motorcycle mama. She had him off balance, intrigued and more interested than he cared to admit. Her former boyfriend had his curiosity pumped.

He gave up the attempt to keep his tone neutral. "We're eating at a bowling alley?"

"Kendrick is a busy man. He's always doing two or three things at once. Tonight, he'll eat dinner, bowl and visit with me all at the same time. Since I've known him, he's worked two, sometimes three, jobs."

"When does he write?"

"At night. He usually coordinates odd occupations with his writing, claiming he's getting paid to do his research. He chooses work related to whatever he's writing."

Summer spoke of her former boyfriend without bitterness, as if she admired the man's ambition and talents. Still, he couldn't forget the catch in her voice when she'd admitted her relationship with Kendrick lacked passion. After holding her in his arms, Craig knew she possessed a zest for life. She'd trembled against him and her husky voice had vibrated with a come-hither contralto.

Had Kendrick blamed her for his own failings? Or was the man just too self-involved to give Summer what she'd needed?

He curled his fingers around the steering wheel, then straightened them. Her past hurts didn't matter. Her feelings made no difference to him.

None whatsoever.

So why couldn't he stop thinking about her? He should concentrate on the stalker's identity, keep his focus on protecting her to keep the babies safe. Nothing else should concern him.

He forced his words back to business. "What kind of work does Kendrick use for reference material?"

"His odd jobs are never glamorous. He's a janitor on the night shift at newspapers or police stations. He claims the uniform makes him invisible and people say things they'd never reveal in an interview."

A man who wrote horror stories. A man who sneaked around at night. A man who hung around police stations. What better cover for a stalker?

She must have glimpsed his suspicion. Annoyance flashed in her eyes, but she squared her shoulders. "I don't care what the statistics say, Kendrick wouldn't do this to me."

He saw no reason to argue, especially before he'd met the man. "What about your uncle Bob?"

As he turned off the freeway toward smoggy L.A., she snorted in derision, but he caught her carefully watching in the side mirror to make sure they hadn't picked up a tail. "Uncle Bob's primary interest is his next drink. Besides, in the past ten years, he hasn't been sober long enough to ride a motorcycle."

Summer took the bag of Chinese food onto her lap, and Craig turned into the lot of the bowling alley and parked. "Are you sure they'll let you bring food inside?"

She hesitated to leave the vehicle and watched a stranger who'd pulled into the lot right behind them. But when the man reached into the trunk and retrieved his bowling bag, she turned back to Craig as if her watchfulness was mere idle curiosity. "Kendrick has a special arrangement with the manager. He mentions the bowling alley in most of his books, and it's good publicity."

They hurried inside to be greeted by the sounds of balls rolling and bumping down the alleys, some striking pins, others slamming into the gutters with jarring thuds. A teenage league had spread over half the lanes while others were reserved for walk-ins like themselves.

Frowning at the smoke and the music blaring from the jukebox beside the pinball machines and pool tables, Craig longed for the crisp, quiet air of the Pacific, yet he was anxious to meet Summer's old boyfriend.

"We need to rent shoes," Summer suggested.

Craig shook his head. "This isn't a date. I just want to ask the guy some questions."

"Kendrick will be more relaxed if we throw a few balls."

Her former boyfriend sounded like quite a character, and he wasn't sure if he approved of the obvious fondness in her tone when she spoke of him. Several minutes later, after he met the man, Craig's mind filled with sour thoughts. He'd expected a squirrelly nerd behind horn-rimmed glasses. Kendrick was a muscular five foot eleven with thick black hair, a clean-cut smile and a surfer's tan.

The men shook hands, and Craig noted Kendrick's strong grip and his head-to-toe evaluation of Summer's escort. From Summer's remarks about Kendrick's self-absorption, he hadn't expected her ex-boyfriend to size him up like this. Irritation at Kendrick's possessive attitude flared in Craig, causing him to wonder if perhaps Summer's other perceptions were off, as well. Was Kendrick more upset about the breakup than she realized? Did he want her back?

Telling himself he needed additional answers about Kendrick's feelings for Summer, Craig deliberately sat close beside her and casually looped his arm over her shoulder. Kendrick's eyes widened, and his lips twitched in neither smile nor grimace, making him hard to read.

Summer handed Kendrick the bag of food. "We brought dinner."

Unreasonably irritated that she'd given their food to Kendrick, Craig masked his annoyance.

Kendrick reached into the bag of food and helped himself to an egg roll. After taking a huge bite, he set it down, ambled to his bowling ball and finished the last frame of his game. Without glancing in their direction, he gulped down the rest of his egg roll while updating the automatic computerized scoring system.

Summer removed the rest of the food from the bag,

the green in her eyes brightening with interest as she glanced at Kendrick. "So what's your exciting news?"

What would it take to get her to be as interested in Craig's business?

Kendrick's chest puffed at her question. "I'm finally going to produce a movie—co-produce, actually."

Craig dipped an egg roll into sweet and sour sauce and paused with the food on the way to his mouth. Annoyance had reduced his appetite. Didn't Kendrick have anyone else to celebrate his good fortunes with besides Summer?

Forcing enthusiasm into his voice, Craig tried to look impressed. "Congratulations."

Summer's eyes shone. "That's wonderful! You've worked so hard for this opportunity. Tell us about the movie."

At her enthusiasm over Kendrick's accomplishment, Craig bit into his egg roll so hard his jaw ached.

"I sneaked in the back door. When Ron Kilmar wanted to buy the movie rights to my book—"

"Ron Kilmar?" Summer broke in, her voice rising with excitement.

Even Craig recognized the name as one of the biggest in Hollywood. So not only was her boyfriend attractive and famous, now he would most likely become even wealthier. He almost choked on his egg roll at the realization he was jealous, not of Kendrick's success, but of Summer's high regard for the other man.

Luckily, she had a prior obligation to him. With Summer pregnant with his children, she was unable to take up where she'd left off with Kendrick. Satisfaction coursed through him, but he couldn't help wondering if she was sorry she'd agreed to be a surrogate.

"...and as part of the deal, I insisted on co-producing."

Kendrick knew how to use leverage all right, but Craig, overriding his jealousy, couldn't fault him for fulfilling a lifelong ambition. In his own import-export business the proper use of leverage often made the difference between average earnings or huge success. Timing and courage plus knowing when to go for maximum profits took sharp instincts.

Clearly, the writer was talented in his field. Craig had learned that his books often made the *New York Times* bestsellers list. For him to have secured the title of co-producer showed he had the clout and the business savvy to make the most of his publishing success.

Craig should have had more faith in Summer's judgment. Despite his irritation with the man's boasting, he realized many women would consider Kendrick husband material.

With Summer beside Craig, Kendrick's excluding Craig from the conversation might be accidental. However, Kendrick's refusal to glance Craig's way since his initial appraisal struck Craig as odd. And telling. Perhaps the jealousy went two ways. After all, Craig had invited himself on their date.

Niggling suspicions remained about Kendrick's feelings toward Summer. Why hadn't Kendrick commented on her appearance? Why hadn't he asked about her? Or about why she'd brought another man to what he must have thought of as a date?

"Which book are you filming?" Summer asked, then held up her hand. "No wait. Let me guess. *Blood Lust* was always my favorite."

Craig wasn't a horror fan and he fought a frown at the distasteful title. *"Blood Lust?"*

Kendrick ignored him and the censure in his tone. "That's the one. We're casting next week. Kilmar already has several big stars angling for the lead."

Summer scooped some shrimp and fried veggies onto plates and handed each of them dinner before turning to Craig. "Blood Lust is about a woman whose husband never returned from a secret CIA mission. As she seeks the reason for her husband's death, she terrorizes each person in different ways, preying on their weaknesses until they break."

Kendrick paced and talked as he ate. "We have a hundred-million dollar budget, which means the special-effects people can go all out. Kilmar already has marketing working on a dynamite ad campaign. 'Entertainment Tonight' wants an interview, but my agent is stalling until I move into a new place."

As Summer's smile clearly indicated her pleasure over Kendrick's success, Craig's inherent dislike of the man escalated. Even her tone softened. "Sounds like you're on your way, Kendrick. I'll be able to say I knew you when."

"Yeah, you'll be able to say you knew me when I was a jerk. Come back, Summer. We could be good together. I'll be able to treat you in style."

Stunned, outraged, Craig stopped chewing. Kendrick had apologized, asked her to come back and tried to bribe her all without missing a bite of his egg roll. Had the man no manners or sensitivity? Didn't he realize some conversations should be held in private?

Summer tensed then chuckled, apparently accustomed to dealing with his brusque demeanor. "You'll be so wrapped up in your movie, you won't notice whether I'm there or not. When's your next book due?"

At her refusal of Kendrick's offer, Craig's defenses subsided and relief washed away some of his tension. His mood lightened as she smoothly turned the conversation from the personal back to Kendrick, who was more than happy to talk about his work. The self-absorbed writer-producer seemed unaware she hadn't answered his plea.

Kendrick picked up his bowling ball and took the left lane. "I've stopped writing books. However, turning in my screenplay on time will be a tight squeeze. At least the story comes almost straight from my first book." He walked smoothly down the lane, never breaking stride as he spoke nonstop, finally releasing the ball in one practiced motion. "I just haven't figured out yet when the villain should kill the fetus."

Craig's stomach lurched. Summer's face turned white until her eyes were two large green pools of fear. Her lips tightened as if holding back her repugnance.

"Moving the story from book format to the big screen has its own difficulties. Do you think I should wait until after the kid's born and the mother becomes attached? Or would it be worse if I poisoned the mother slowly? I was cleaning the autopsy room at the hospital last week and overheard the forensics guys speculating. Certain poisons in small doses pass through the placenta and kill the fetus without the mother being permanently harmed.''

Kendrick's bowling ball veered to the left and struck light on the head pin, leaving two pins standing. He picked up the spare on his second ball before returning.

"Summer, your face is as white as chalk dust. You know the story. What's wrong? You never minded me talking about the grisly stuff before."

Craig rubbed her arm. Summer spoke through gritted teeth. "I've never been pregnant before."

"Oh, gosh." Kendrick reddened, looking from her to Craig and then at her still-flat stomach. "I didn't know. Why didn't you say something? I wouldn't have asked you to come back if ."

Craig glared.

Kendrick kept talking. "I mean, I don't care whether you got knocked up. Just get rid of it, and I'll take you back."

Summer gasped. "I couldn't—"

"I don't think the lady's interested." Craig contained his sudden longing to smash Kendrick's gleaming white teeth down his throat. Kendrick's suggestion for her to terminate the pregnancy had him ready for a good fight. While he wasn't worried about controlling his violent urge, that he even considered going to such extremes was unsettling. "Did you ever think she'd rather have a baby than you?"

"I—I..." Kendrick stammered. "I'm not into having a family. Summer knows that. Creativity demands that I focus on my work."

"Well then, we'll leave you to it," Craig said grimly, letting none of his thoughts about rearranging Kendrick's face show on his own.

Summer breathed deeply. "Hey, let's not forget why we're here. Besides, I'm okay. That stuff he said about killing the fetus kind of got to me. I'd forgotten that aspect of the plot. Must be the hormones."

"Don't apologize," Craig said. "My stomach curdled and I'm not pregnant."

She squeezed his hand. "You don't understand. Kendrick always talks out his plots with me."

"Not anymore, he doesn't."

Her eyes pleaded with him to calm down. "This is the first time I reacted that way, so don't blame him, okay?"

As much as he longed to launch himself at Kendrick and shake the man, he didn't allow his feelings to mar his cool demeanor. After Kendrick's crack about getting rid of his children, why did she defend the creep?

As if nothing out of the ordinary had happened, Kendrick jerked his head toward the lane. "You going to take your turn or what?"

Craig massaged Summer's neck with one hand. "*I'm* going to make sure Summer is all right. Feel free to take my turn."

He supposed he should have been shocked when Kendrick did just that.

"Are you okay?" Craig asked Summer, pleased when color returned to her face.

"Kendrick's embarrassed. He doesn't know how to apologize."

"The brilliant writer has never heard the words

'I'm sorry'?'' Craig rubbed her neck and her shoulders, marveling at the silky smoothness of her skin. ''Do you always make excuses for him?''

Summer bit her bottom lip. ''Is that what I was doing?''

She stared down the bowling lane absently. At first, he thought she was watching Kendrick, but as Craig peered into her eyes, he changed his mind. She wasn't looking at Kendrick; she was looking through him.

What was going through her head? Was she reevaluating her relationship? Questioning past judgments? Reliving conversations? He knew the routine. How many times had he wished he could recant a harsh word that he'd spoken in anger to Linda? Why hadn't he given her more of his time?

He recalled all the times she had come into his home office to tell him he'd been working too long, too late. He hadn't heeded her wishes often enough. They'd had so little time together, and he'd spent the years building the import side of his business, often traveling, always working. He'd been out to conquer the world. So many possibilities, so much to do. He'd always thought he could slow down later, spend more time with her later. But time had run out. Since his wife's death, he'd beaten himself up for the moments he'd wasted.

He wouldn't make those mistakes again. Not since he'd discovered the possessive nature of his feelings toward Summer. Not only did he intend to protect his babies, he vowed to spend time getting to know her better. She'd stirred feelings inside him he hadn't felt in years, and he promised himself he would explore them.

Starting with her lips. He knew just what to do with those slightly parted lips. Nip them, tease them, coax them until she yielded.

Suddenly, he couldn't stand to share her any longer with her ex-boyfriend in the smoke-filled bowling alley. He wanted to go someplace fresh and clean.

He glanced at her. "Why don't we get out of here? I've heard enough."

She averted her gaze, but steely determination entered her whisper. "Not yet. I want to know where Kendrick was the day I was attacked in the park."

Did her statement suggest she suddenly saw Kendrick in a new light? Or was she simply trying to prove to Craig that Kendrick wasn't stalking her?

When she asked Kendrick his whereabouts that day, he couldn't remember. Either the man was the best liar Craig had ever seen, or he was telling the truth and really couldn't remember, or he had a split personality. Craig found all three possibilities disturbing.

As they removed their rented bowling shoes, Kendrick reached into his pocket and pulled out a crumpled napkin. "Harry Pibbs is looking for you. He called me last week."

Curious. Why would her former boss be calling her old boyfriend?

"What did he want?" Summer asked.

"Don't know," Kendrick mumbled, barely looking away from his score.

Maybe Summer was right. The man didn't know how to apologize. When he wasn't bragging about his work, he certainly was the awkward toad in social situations.

Kendrick shrugged. "You know I never answer the phone when I'm working. Harry left this message on my machine. He said you should call him back. He said it was urgent."

THE VISIT WITH Kendrick had sapped Summer's energy. She pretended to nod off, and Craig drove straight home. She couldn't blame her fatigue on her pregnancy. She knew better. Seeing Kendrick again had forced her to relive her old fear that she wasn't worthy of being loved. Every time she'd glanced at Craig and found his speculative gaze on her had increased her discomfort.

Sure, Kendrick had asked her to come back to him, but he hadn't blinked an eye when she'd changed the subject instead of answering. He didn't really want her, not enough to fight for her, not enough to try to convince her to stay. Certainly not enough for him to make an effort to talk about more than his favorite topic—himself. Craig's witnessing the entire scene had made her humiliation complete.

Why had she put up with Kendrick's self-absorbed idiosyncrasies? What was lacking in her that she'd sought his approval?

Ever since her parents died, Summer had felt guilty. If only she'd been good, God wouldn't have taken them away from her. Then her grandfather died, and she knew she had to be the best little girl in the world or she'd lose Gran, too. As an adult, she knew her childhood fears were irrational. But she couldn't erase the years of trying to be perfect. If she was good enough, nothing bad would happen. If she was good enough, Kendrick would have paid more attention to her, loved her. Being good meant putting his wishes before her own. If they hadn't broken up, there'd be nothing of herself left.

After Kendrick, she'd known she would never marry. She'd given all she had to the relationship and her efforts had fallen painfully, humiliatingly short. He still didn't love her and she no longer trusted her judgment. Each man would leave her—just as her parents and grandfather had, just as Kendrick had let her go, just as Craig would once he got what she had to give him—his babies.

At least Craig was honest with her. He might be physically attracted to her, but he'd made his priority clear from the start. His first concern was for his babies. He'd only put up with her until she delivered his children, then she'd be a footnote in his life.

She hadn't been as honest with him. Her stomach knotted. There was no telling how he'd react when he found out what she'd done. Deception didn't come easy to her—certainly not without piles of guilt. Of course, after he had the babies he wanted so desperately, her lies wouldn't matter.

Thankfully, once they reached Craig's house, he didn't question her about her past. After they went inside, he left her in privacy to call her former boss, Harry, while he went upstairs and changed, then escaped to the backyard pool.

After her chat with Harry, she'd fully intended to go upstairs to her room and sleep. She knew, though, that Craig had to be curious about her conversation and she could use his clearheaded logic to help mull over what Harry had said, so she joined Craig by the pool.

The sun had set. A neighbor's late-dinner barbecue with its pleasant scent of steaks smoking on the grill accompanied the chirp of crickets. Summer settled onto a lounge chair and waited for Craig to surface in the pool, appreciative of the underwater lights that highlighted his silhouette.

He swam with long, powerful strokes, his legs churning bubbles. Breaking the surface with his back to her, he sneaked a breath and dived under, frolicking like a dolphin and as at home in the water as a shark.

The disparity of the two images—dolphin and shark—weren't contradictory in Craig Banks. He knew how to play, yet he never lost a razor-sharp edge that could take him to the top of his chosen field. Although he'd rarely mentioned his business, she sensed that after his wife died, his business goals had taken a back seat to his grief. Knowing he needed to provide for the children had spurred him on to rebuild his life.

He burst to the surface, spied her and waved. "Come on in."

Baring all the skin a swimsuit revealed would set the wrong tone for the conversation she had in mind. Besides, she'd exposed enough of herself to him today. To be close was to invite rejection. "No, thanks. Just watching you tired me out."

To her relief, he didn't insist, but swam to the edge. "How are you feeling? You looked tapped out in the car."

"I'm fine now."

Craig flattened his hands on the pool deck and, in one easy motion, pulled himself out of the water. She looked away from all his rippling bronzed flesh, but not before the image seared into her brain and heated her face.

Backlit by the blue water of the pool, he cut a dashing image of broad shoulders, muscular biceps and firm pecs. A sudden nebulous desire rose in her—to be close, to touch—a childish longing honed by a woman's sensuality.

Craig plucked a towel from the back of a chair. The clean scent of him wafted to her on a soft breeze and stirred the curly hairs that undulated with each movement of his arm. She ached to smooth his tangled hair from his eyes, take the towel from his hands and dry him. Slowly. Sensuously.

Keeping her gaze above his flat waist proved impossible. He wore a black, itty-bitty swimsuit that covered him just enough to fire her imagination.

Closing the distance between them, he wrapped the towel around his waist, pulled up a chair and took her hand.

She wished she could pull her hand back without causing a fuss. His touch had her feeling trapped and antsy and turned on. The heat in his eyes told her he was noticing her like a man who wanted a woman. And he was all man. An enticing, undeniably sexy man.

He was too close for her not to inhale the mingled scent of chlorine and masculine male power. His bare chest, broad shoulders and muscular thighs had her swallowing hard. The heat from his touch traveled up her arm and down into the pit of her stomach. He focused a sudden interest on her mouth.

His lips claimed hers tenderly, gently, coaxing and

teasing until she leaned into him. As if sensing the exact moment she surrendered to her racing desire, he pulled her onto his lap, deepening the kiss.

Her hands wound around his neck until her fingers threaded his thick wet hair. His chest was damp and hot, his kiss both more intense and more gentle than she'd expected. The biggest surprise was her reaction to him.

Nerves pulsed with excitement. For once, she wasn't worried if she pleased a man. She wasn't concerned if their noses bumped or whether she'd just brushed her teeth. All practical thoughts and insecurities vanished.

She was too busy savoring her own out-of-control reactions. Puzzled and a bit afraid of the intense fire he'd kindled with his kiss, she jerked back. "I need to tell you about Harry."

He leaned forward to kiss her again. "Tell me later."

She braced her palm on his chest and allowed herself to look up at him, almost wishing she didn't have to. Up close, she could see the light in his dark gray eyes and a soft smile caressing his mouth. He looked like a man who knew far too much about women, far too much about her.

She held his gaze, didn't even blink. "This is important."

He shrugged, the corner of his mouth lifting in amused resignation. "So what did Harry say?"

"He was concerned when I didn't cash my last paycheck." Before Craig could ask, she explained, "I was afraid to return to my apartment. I couldn't have the mail forwarded out of fear the stalker might trace me.''

''Did Harry mention where he was the day the biker attacked you?''

Talking to him while he sat there bare chested, wasn't easy, especially after he'd just kissed her and heated her blood. She didn't want to ask him to cover up for fear of revealing her weakness. ''Harry said he worked right through the lunch hour. It's doubtful anyone was with him during that time. We'd usually let the service pick up the messages while the secretaries all lunched out together.''

''So he doesn't have an alibi, either.''

She rubbed her chin. ''Unless he answered the phone. I suppose I could check with the service tomorrow.''

His eyes narrowed. ''So Harry called Kendrick just to find out where you were?''

''Kendrick misled us. Harry called him, but when Kendrick didn't answer, he never left a message. Instead, Kendrick went to talk with Harry in person.''

''Kendrick lied?''

She shrugged. ''More like he omitted the truth.''

''So Kendrick visited Harry the same day you were attacked in the park.''

''Yes, but don't jump to conclusions. Kendrick has always been a little strange.''

One brow shot skyward. ''A little? Don't you think it odd Kendrick omitted telling you he visited Harry?''

''Odd, yes. Maybe he cares about me more than he's willing to admit. That could be why he didn't tell us he went to see Harry.''

"I don't understand."

"Maybe Kendrick didn't want to appear as if he missed me."

Craig snorted. "Kendrick is not a man who cares much about appearances. What else did Harry say?"

She didn't want to tell him. She hated revealing her past to Craig for analysis. Not only was her privacy invaded, she felt uncomfortable seeing her relationship through his eyes. Yet he had a right to know, though she could put off the worst of the news for a few moments more.

"Harry was looking for me for several reasons. One was the check I never cashed. The second was his worry over me. And last, he wanted to invite me to a party."

Craig's eyes narrowed and his voice hardened as if they'd never shared that kiss. "What did you say?"

She avoided a direct answer, picking a spot past his ear to stare at while refusing to let her gaze follow the trickle of water from his forehead. "Every year, the firm throws a bash for its employees, clients and suppliers. Anyone Harry owes a favor to is invited."

Craig frowned. "You don't work there anymore."

"Harry hoped to lure me back. He reminded me that I could still work for him part-time while I attend law school at night."

"Law school?"

She winced at the surprise in Craig's tone. Did he think her incapable of becoming a lawyer or simply lacking in ambition? Either way left a bad taste in her mouth.

Anger at his implied insult gave her the courage to

look him straight in the eye. "I was accepted into Stanford."

"You couldn't swing the finances with Gran's bills," he guessed, his tone sympathetic.

She suddenly realized that his surprise at her trying for law school hadn't been denigrating her intelligence or ambition, but merely an accurate assessment of her inability to pay the bills. "Gran doesn't know. I'd appreciate if you didn't mention it to her."

"I won't." He leaned forward and took her hand, his thumb caressing her palm in a sensual gesture that had her senses thrumming. "You can't accept Harry's party invitation."

"Why not?"

"Are you crazy? You can't put my children in jeopardy."

"My living in fear for the next eight months isn't good for the babies, either."

"But—"

"Look, if I go to the party, we might flush out the stalker. And you'll be there to protect me."

He folded his arms across his chest and shook his head. "You're not going."

She ignored the worry lines radiating from his eyes, the edge in his tone and her churning stomach. "I told Harry I'd bring you as my date."

Chapter Six

After Summer used the shock of her news to slip away, Craig allowed her to escape to her room with a soft good-night. She'd looked sad after seeing Kendrick, but their kiss had put a snap in her step and a sparkle in her eyes. Between her high-voltage kiss that left him aching to accompany her to bed and the bomb she'd just dropped, he was a bit shell-shocked.

Had she gone along with his kiss, hoping to convince him to let her go to the party? But she couldn't have known he intended to kiss her. He hadn't known himself. For all his resolutions to keep his hands off her, he didn't regret kissing her. He could still taste the sweetness of her mouth. Still hear the soft purr of longing at the back of her throat, feel the softness of her breasts and the hardness of her nipples against his chest.

In another moment, he would have had his hand under her shirt and stopping himself would have been nearly impossible. Yet the longer he resisted touching her, the more irresistible the urge became.

The guilt he'd expected to feel from kissing a woman other than his first wife never materialized.

The automatic buffer that had protected him these past few years was gone. A weight he hadn't known he'd been carrying lifted, leaving him light-headed and oddly content.

Perhaps he was simply rationalizing his own response to Summer. In truth, little had held his interest lately. His passion for business had gone down the tubes. Work had become tedious. Without a family, what was the point?

Sure, he'd forced himself to date. While the pleasures of scented skin and affable conversation were very well and good, the women had all seemed alike. Boring.

The only thing that had brought him the slightest pleasure was thinking about his plans for a family. The embryos he and his wife had created still existed after she was gone. Finally, he'd made the decision to hire a surrogate and slowly he'd come out of his funk.

While his interest in business gradually rejuvenated, his interest in women had palled for good. None aroused his interest. He hadn't realized how accustomed he'd become to his empty house. How he'd immersed himself in loneliness. Until Summer had shown up at his front door wearing black leather.

Her arrival had stunned him like a knockout punch. Her proximity alone made his head spin. She actually had him dizzy with her stories and his veins pumping with curiosity. He'd been fighting a bewildering torrent of emotions since the first moment he saw her. Maybe "emotion" was the wrong word. "Reaction" seemed less threatening. Exasperation, irritation, fury, resentment, grudging admiration when she stood up to him. All suffused with the worst case of lust he'd experienced in a very long time.

Their response to each other was mutual. For some crazy reason, she wanted him. He hadn't missed the breathless way she'd leaned into him during their kiss. Afterward, her mouth was moist and swollen from his, her pupils dilated in her flushed face, she'd suddenly looked as if he'd just rocked her safe little world.

He grinned. *No, he certainly wasn't bored.*

He entered the kitchen and poured himself a glass of orange juice while realizing there were all kinds of reasonable explanations for Summer's effect on his senses. For one thing, he hadn't made love to another woman since his wife's death. So all feelings aside, his physical response to Summer was as natural as ice melting during a heat wave.

How she felt about him was another subject. After their argument over whether to attend the party, she was none too pleased with him. She'd stated her argument eloquently and logically, but he hated the idea of using her as bait. Then again, in the back of his mind was the hope that if the stalker believed they were truly married and that Craig would protect her, perhaps he'd back off and the attacks would stop. They should be able to fool a casual observer into believing that they were in love.

He could have sworn she'd taken as much pleasure in their kiss as he had. Yet she'd stopped him with words about the party and Kendrick. Had she been thinking about her old boyfriend while he'd held her? Or had she simply grabbed the first excuse to break free of the passion that consumed her?

A scream, Summer's scream, had him bounding to his feet, sprinting across the kitchen and charging the stairs three at a time in desperation to reach her. Raw nerves cramped his stomach. His heart pounded with dread and pulse-lancing fear.

Had the stalker found her? Was he in the house? Craig should have checked every room when they'd first gotten home. Only he'd been so sure Kendrick was responsible. Could the horror writer have beaten them here and wormed his way past the security alarm before they'd arrived?

Upstairs, Summer had turned on the light. She stood in the hallway, wearing a towel wrapped around her head, gripping the belt of his robe tight at her waist, her face three shades too pale. Water droplets trickled down her neck, and her skin was still damp and dewy from her shower as if she hadn't taken time to dry herself.

She didn't look injured, and a measure of his panic subsided, although adrenaline carried him up the steps with wary intensity. "What's wrong? Are you all right?"

"I laid out fresh underwear on the bed." She gave a weak little laugh, but he didn't miss the slight tremble of her shoulders.

He risked taking one of her icy hands in his to rub some warmth into her. She yanked him toward the guest room.

His gaze fanned over the bed and settled on snips of material, black slivers smaller than confetti. He inhaled a shaky breath. He assumed the material had once been her underwear.

Before he'd worked through the implications that

the stalker had followed her to his home and been in her bedroom, she handed him a slip of paper. His attention riveted on the typed message: "I've been watching," it read, and it was signed, "The Sentry."

"This matches the one you found on your car windshield," he guessed.

She nodded.

He took her into his arms. "We're going to find this creep. You're safe now."

"No," she whispered as she pointed into the room. "I'm not. Neither are the babies." She placed both hands over her womb. "He's found me again. We have to get out of here."

His gaze focused on the sliced underwear and icy fear shimmied down his spine. He could have lost Summer and the babies. As much as he wanted to check the alarm and search the house for the intruder, he wouldn't leave Summer alone. And she was in no shape to go with him.

Summer squeezed his hand so hard his fingers went numb. "He was in the bedroom while I took a shower." Her voice broke. "I shut the bathroom door—but not all the way."

Even if steamy, the clear glass shower stall wouldn't have been protection enough from prying eyes. Her teeth chattered and her jaw clenched as she made an obvious effort to regain her composure.

Her voice cracked. "He was watching me bathe while he sliced the panties. He's sick."

"I'm sorry." For the first time, he had an inkling of how violated she must feel.

He ached to tell her everything would be all right. But how could he when the stalker had actually been in his house? Dark, sinister violence swirled in him. He'd failed to protect his wife from a riptide; he wouldn't fail another woman. He curled his fingers into his palms, vowing to put her safety and the children's first.

Not for one moment did he consider she was making this up. Her voice shook and her icy palms were sweaty. Yet he sensed she didn't want his sympathy. "Did you see him?"

"No." Pain and regret flashed through her eyes.

She jerked away. While he stood helplessly, she pulled the duffel from the closet. "He's likely long gone by now," he tried to reassure her.

Opening and closing drawers, she removed her clothing and dumped items into the bag without bothering to fold, sort or organize. "He could be outside watching us right now, waiting to see what we do and where we go." Her voice rose an octave with desperation. "We can't run blindly. We can't delay, either. I don't know why he didn't kill me. He certainly had the chance."

Her words were cool, rational and practical, yet her voice shook and her hands trembled so badly she couldn't pick up the cosmetics from the bureau, opting instead to brush them into the duffel with her forearm. That she was shaken to her core, he didn't doubt.

After his initial relief that she wasn't harmed, his own reactions were more delayed. Stunned, his first instinct was to protect her and the babies. Should he check the house? Despite his reassurance, the stalker could still be inside. But he didn't dare leave her unguarded.

As he stared at the shreds of black material, he girded himself to face facts. The stalker had been in the house, in this room. The sick bastard had watched Summer shower, left a note, cut up her underwear. Why?

Fear, anger and desperation for her and the children surged in him like waves in a stormy sea. The stalker hadn't hurt her but instead had frightened her half to death. "Maybe his intent isn't to kill you."

"Maybe he's toying with me like a cat with a cornered mouse. I'm not sticking around to find out." Her head jerked up and the towel fell partway off her head, though not enough for him to ascertain her hair color. She grabbed a pair of jeans, a shirt and a brunette wig and went into the bathroom to change. She emerged, looking like another stranger. This time, she'd outlined her eyes with black. Her lashes looked longer than usual. A headband over her forehead kept the latest wig in place.

She'd gone to great lengths to alter her appearance. But neither her numerous disguises nor a change in jobs and living arrangements had prevented the stalker from finding her. They had to do better. He wasn't sure what he could come up with that she hadn't already tried herself.

"Perhaps we should go to the police," he suggested, bracing himself for her protest.

"No." A fierce burning sprang into her eyes. After placing toiletries into a side compartment, she zipped the duffel bag, adding emphasis to her words. "I told you I think the stalker might have a connection inside the police department. When we went to court, I had to give my name and address. You did, too. Maybe the stalker picked up my trail from police records.''

''Suppose you're wrong? We could be avoiding the people that can help us the most.''

She shook her head, venting anger. ''Even if I'm wrong, what could we tell them? That someone cut up my underwear?'' She threw up her hands in frustration. ''I can't even give a description.''

Craig leaned against the doorjamb, hoping she wouldn't belatedly realize the stalker might still be in the house and he'd stationed himself in the doorway to protect her. ''Kendrick likely has connections at police departments. He was in town the day of the attack and has the knowledge to stalk you. Maybe the police could assign someone to watch him.''

Slinging the bag's strap onto her shoulder, she looked over at him, her eyes now brown and too wise for a woman her age. ''We can discuss this while you pack.''

He backed toward his room, seeing the merit in her suggestion. She followed, and he locked them inside. While she plopped onto his bed, he tossed articles of clothing into a suitcase.

''I told you,'' she said, ''Kendrick isn't the stalker. I know him. He has a gentle soul.''

''Right.'' He threw a swimsuit into the case. ''His gentle soul suggested you get rid of my children.''

''I never said he wasn't selfish.'' She sighed, glanced at the clothes he'd packed and frowned. ''Unless you're planning on adding some shirts and slacks, you're going to look mighty peculiar in only a swimsuit, tie and socks.''

''Very funny.'' Craig raked his fingers through his

hair and shot her a wry glance as he realized he was more shaken by the intrusion into his home than he'd realized. The stalker had been right there with her and he hadn't known. He strode to his closet and threw several shirts and slacks into his bag before removing his computer notebook from its case. "I'll find us a place to stay."

"Where are we going? Wherever we stay has to be someplace not easily traced to you. I can't leave the area. Despite what Gran said, I have to stay close enough to look in on her every few days."

Craig plugged his modem into the phone line. "I've a friend who's on vacation in Europe. If he didn't rent his house, we might stay there."

"What about leaving here undetected?"

"Call a cab and have them meet us on the corner of Fifth and Morgan Streets. We'll sneak across the backyard."

She'd stopped packing, and he sensed her gaze on him while he typed. "And then what?"

"Let me worry about that."

"I don't think so."

He was talking, typing and listening, but her sharp tone grabbed his attention. "Huh?"

She folded her arms over her chest, lifted her head and stared him straight in the eye, every inch of her stiffened in protest. "If you think I came here to turn over the decision making to you so I didn't have to worry my little head…"

Her words were a challenge, thrown down like a gauntlet, and he stepped toward her. "Hey, I didn't say—"

"Just because my life is at stake—"

"Okay, okay. I didn't mean that the way it sounded. I just want to protect you and the babies. I'm sorry. Can we leave now and I'll explain on the way?"

She didn't back down an inch, yet her tone softened. "I'm sorry, too. I shouldn't have snapped at you, but I'm edgy, knowing he's found me again."

After Craig E-mailed his friend, they hurried out the back door, through the yard and down a neighboring street. He had to fight his instinct to urge her to run, fearing the stress of the past hours combined with too much physical strain could have grave consequences for his babies.

Summer had phoned for the cab and it waited for them on the corner. Craig handed their luggage to the driver and directed him to take them to the bus station. Summer nodded her approval. Many buses would leave every hour and make tracking them difficult. During the ride, he couldn't help craning his neck to see if a car was following. He spied no one who seemed interested in them and took a measure of relief in the knowledge they seemed to have fled undetected.

Craig paid the taxi driver and hurried her into the bus terminal, surprised and grateful the place was so busy at ten o'clock at night. Yet under the bright fluorescent lights, he felt exposed. Summer, wearing jeans and a casual blouse, fitted right into the crowd, but he was a little overdressed in a designer polo shirt and slacks. Still, there was nothing he could do to disguise himself now.

After taking a bus schedule from a counter display, he led Summer to a bench in a less crowded area by a side door—just in case they needed to make a quick exit. Remembering she wanted to be consulted, he held the schedule between them. "It's decision time. *We* have several choices."

"Where's your friend's house?"

"Malibu."

At her raised brows and pleased expression, Craig didn't bother containing his grin. Even with the danger they faced, the thought of hiding out with Summer in the posh neighborhood by the ocean had his blood thrumming. He'd always enjoyed the sand and the sun, the tang of salt on his skin and the roar of the surf in his ears.

Summer restrained a whistle. With all the movie stars living around L.A., homes along the Pacific were expensive, but Malibu was one of the more exclusive areas. She hadn't realized Craig traveled in such elite circles. No doubt he found her blue-collar background and odd modes of dress unappealing.

She wondered what he'd thought to find his new wife roaring up his driveway in her black leather motorcycle outfit? She bit back a grin as she recalled the priceless expression on his face when she'd told that cop the leather was his idea.

Her urge to grin faded. Being on the run again was no picnic, but at least this time she wasn't alone. She intended to do her part in keeping the babies safe. She owed Craig that much. Maybe, just maybe, she could make up in some small way for the secret she still kept from him.

Tucking a strand of the wig behind her ear, she peered at the schedule. "We could take the first bus heading up the coast to L.A., head inland near Buena

Park and pick up a rental car or completely change directions and go to Mission Viejo.''

"Why don't we go to Anaheim? We'll stop at Logan Gate Mall. I'll have someone at my company drop off a car for us.''

Her brows knitted. "It's the middle of the night.''

"Logan Gate Mall is open twenty-four hours a day. The place caters to Japanese tourists who haven't adjusted to the time change after a red-eye flight, movie stars who party all night and regular Joes who work the night shift but want to shop before sleeping all day. Besides, my people are awake. We do a lot of business in the Far East, so the night shift is on.''

Craig handed her money to purchase the bus tickets, then he used his cell phone to make arrangements for the car. He was still on the phone when she returned, so she dug into her pocket for a quarter and called Gran from a bank of pay phones. She hated to wake her up this late, but she didn't know when she'd next have the opportunity to call.

The phone rang three times before someone picked up the receiver.

"Hello," a man answered in a gravelly voice.

Poor Gran. Uncle Bob must have returned and she'd put him up for the night. With the nurse and Gran and her brother in the small apartment, they must be getting on one another's nerves.

"Uncle Bob?''

"This is Harry Pibbs." The man cleared his throat and the rough tone was replaced by a friendlier one. "Is that you, Summer? Where have you been?''

What was Gran's attorney and Summer's former boss doing in Gran's apartment? What had happened to the nurse? She gripped the phone more tightly, her nerves screaming. "What's wrong? Is Gran all right?"

"She's fine. She caught the nurse pilfering a Wedgwood vase, the blue one she picked up on a trip to Jamaica that she keeps in the—"

"I know where she keeps the Wedgwood, Harry." She couldn't contain her worry. Here he was rattling on about a Wedgwood vase when her heart was beating madly. "What are you doing there?"

"I'm afraid that's privileged attorney-client information."

"You're sure Gran is okay? How's her ankle?"

Harry sighed. "I'll put her on and she can tell you herself."

"I'm just making a living will," her grandmother said. "No cause for alarm, dear."

At Gran's reassurance, her racing heart resumed a normal beat. "How's the ankle?"

"I'll be up to snuff in a few more days."

"If that nurse didn't work out, why didn't you hire another one?"

"Now, Summer, I may be an old bat, but I'm not senile. The nurse was stealing." Gran sniffed. "I won't use that firm again. I found the Wedgwood in her purse and fired her on the spot."

"Why were you looking in her purse?"

"That's neither here nor there. The important thing is that I'm fine." Gran scolded Summer as if she were still a child who had forgotten her manners, making her feel foolish for her worries. "Freddy, the dear boy, stops in once a day to look in on me. The ankle is almost as good as new. I may be dancing by to-morrow night at Harry's party."

"I'm glad to hear that." Inviting Gran was nice of Harry, but then she was a client of his firm, and although she didn't throw him much business, she'd employed Harry for her legal affairs ever since Summer's parents had died. Back then, Harry's business had been foundering, and losing just one client could have bankrupted the teetering firm.

"We'll pick you up about seven."

"No need, dear. I have my own date."

Summer grinned. "You do?"

"Freddy's going to take me. I can't wait to see the look on Mabel's face when I introduce him," Gran crowed gleefully.

Gran and Harry's wife, Mabel, had been in first grade together. Trouble had started when both women had dated the same boy in seventh grade. Summer thought that after all these years the women would have put aside their rivalry, but they relished the chance to show each other up. Mabel was forever bragging about her "young" husband, who was at least a decade younger than Mabel. Now Gran would show up with a man even younger. Summer sighed. Who was she to interfere in their fun?

"Great. I'll see you tomorrow night."

CRAIG AND SUMMER sat side by side in the front of a bus that reeked of stale air. As soon as the driver started the motor and turned on the air-conditioning, the slight nausea in her stomach vanished.

Craig sat with his laptop across his knees, but so far he'd been ignoring the machine ever since he'd used it at his house. Instead, he tilted their seats back, draped one arm over her shoulder and encouraged her to use his chest for a headrest.

"Tired?" he asked.

"I should be. I'm too keyed up to sleep." Her body was pumped with adrenaline—first from learning the stalker had watched her shower, then from the flight from Craig's home, and finally her worry over Gran.

The bus driver pulled out of the terminal. After a glance in the driver's rearview mirror didn't reveal even one set of headlights in pursuit, the tension eased from her shoulders. "How long until we reach Anaheim?"

"About an hour and fifteen minutes. If you're not tired, I'd like to hear about your previous run-ins with the stalker."

She hated discussing her past, but she must. Although she knew her privacy was once again about to be plundered, she shoved her feelings to a back corner. The babies' safety was more important than maintaining her privacy or her pride.

Turning sideways, she looked at him in the dim light of the passing streetlights. "The first time I noticed something wrong was after I'd returned from a visit to Gran's house. I opened my refrigerator. It was empty. Totally cleaned out without even so much as an ice cube in the freezer."

Puzzlement entered his tone. "You'd been robbed?"

"That would have been preferable to the mess I found in my bathroom. Every item from the fridge had been opened and tossed, smashed or broken in the tub, sink and commode. Eggshells stuck to the walls and ceiling. Ketchup sprayed on the mirror, broken glass bottles strewn on the floor with meat, cheese, veggies, fruits. You name it—pieces or chunks were smeared across my bathroom. The entire apartment reeked for days.''

"Did you call the police?''

She shook her head, thinking how calmly she could speak when her heart still rattled with fear. "Maybe I should have. The incident was so bizarre I was sure some crackhead had broken in. And wouldn't be back.'' She licked her lips. "I was wrong.''

"What happened next?''

The bus stopped. No one got on, but she waited for people to get off before she continued, her palms clammy at the memory. "I went into my bedroom several weeks later. A bloody message dripped from the wall above my bed.''

"What did it say?''

Her stomach tied into a thick knot. "Loser!''

"That's all?''

"It didn't make any sense to me, either. This time, I called the cops.'' Goose bumps stippled her arms and she shivered. Waiting for the police to come had been frightening. "They took about an hour to show up. When they arrived, I took them to the bedroom to show them the wall. But the writing was gone.''

He scratched his head. "I don't understand.''

"Neither did the cops. The officers thought I was nuts. I called Kendrick. He said that there are substances that disappear after they've been in contact with air—like the disappearing ink kids use to stain clothes and fool their moms before it disappears.''

Craig rubbed his hand up and down her arm, banishing the worst of her chill. "What else did Kendrick say?"

"He offered to come over, but he really wanted me to go to his place. He even offered to sleep on the couch until we got used to one another again—he meant until he wormed his way back into my good graces. I didn't go." He took her hand and squeezed. She relished the solid warmth of him, the genuine comfort he gave her. That he didn't pressure her gave her the courage to go on. "I moved after I found chicken blood all over my sheets."

"Chicken blood?"

She shuddered. "That's what forensics said. Finding the blood was the last straw. I was petrified. The cops told me moving and changing jobs might be the only way to lose the stalker. So I quit working for Harry, went to work for your attorney's firm and moved into another apartment."

"He found you again?"

"Not right away. I thought I was safe. When I went home and found my pillow shredded and feathers glued to my television screen, I knew I had to do something drastic."

"You went to the clinic and let the doctors plant the embryos inside you."

She squeezed his hand tight, willing him to follow and understand her reasoning. "I was desperate to disappear. With the money you provided, I wouldn't have to work. I could hide. I was so careful. I used a fake name, wore wigs and never went to my usual haunts. I intended to lie on a couch, get fat with the twins and rest. Just in case he did find me, I stored a bag in the locker at the bus station. I didn't tell anyone where I'd moved except the police, who insisted on knowing my address. I didn't even tell Gran.''

He didn't pull his hand from hers—an encouraging sign. When he spoke, she braced for the fire-breathing anger he'd displayed the last time they'd discussed her putting his babies in jeopardy.

His tone remained calm, thoughtful. "That's why you think the stalker is working with the police?"

She nodded, wondering if he had any idea how frightened she'd been. "The first time and place I saw him since I moved was in the park.'' A shiver slid up her spine and wedged in her neck until the hair there prickled. "I knew then that he wouldn't stop looking until he found me.''

"He never physically threatened you, did he?"

"In the park, he raised a baton over my head like he meant to bash my skull. I'd consider that physically threatening.''

Craig wasn't being argumentative. He sounded as if he believed her but was puzzled by something he couldn't quite figure out. "If he wanted you dead, why would he watch you take a shower—''

"While he cut up my underwear? I don't know. He's sick. Nothing makes sense.''

Despite the chills weaving a web of ice down her spine, she sensed his thoughts churning. Did he think Kendrick had tried to scare her into returning? Deep down, she knew Craig didn't buy her faith in Kendrick, so she kept quiet.

They switched to the car at the mall without any trouble, and she dozed while Craig drove up the coast to Malibu. When he shut off the car's engine, she opened her eyes. A balmy breeze wafted the sharp tangy scent of the sea her way. Invigorated, she stepped from the car, her gaze sweeping past the three-story contemporary house to the more spectacular view below.

Moonlight disappeared in the inky waves that lapped the rocky shoreline. Several huge boulders rose up from the sloshing waters, their dark shadows a stain on the flat sea.

"The house key is supposed to be under a flowerpot beside the front door." Craig popped the trunk and set their bags on the stoop. A gust of wind whipped around the house. The front door, which should have been locked, blew open.

A pair of sandy footprints led inside.

Chapter Seven

Craig's fingers tightened into fists, matching the knot in her stomach. His voice was brusque, authoritative. "Wait here. I'll check out the house."

A chill wind shimmied over her skin. The cold seeped into her bones. No way was she staying out here in the dark alone. From the fury on Craig's face, the tense set of his shoulders and the hard clench of his jaw, she figured the safest place to be was right behind him.

"I'm going with you."

He spun on his heel to face her, clearly furious she'd given him an argument, but fear rather than defiance must have shown in her expression, because he relented. "Stay close behind me." He handed her the car keys. "At the first sign of trouble, run for the car and lean on the horn to draw the neighbors' attention."

"Got it." She edged closer, using his bulk to protect her from the wind.

As they walked through the front door, a light in the living room flickered on. Summer sucked in her breath, willing the pounding of her heart to subside so she could listen above the roaring in her ears.

Had her stalker gotten here ahead of them? That wasn't possible unless Craig's computer messages had been tracked. She had no idea if such sophisticated technology existed or had just been made up for the movies.

She crossed the threshold on shaking legs and lost her balance on the slippery marble floor. Only Craig's firm grip kept her from falling. At the sound of hurried footsteps and a thump ahead, she peered around Craig into a magnificent living room. Fifteen-foot-high windows gave a wall-to-wall view of the ocean. Leather furniture, free-form sculptures and a Picasso over a massive stone fireplace lent the house a modern ambience.

Off to one side of the room stood a huge fish tank with colorful saltwater fish, and as Summer shifted her gaze past the tank, a slender silhouette moved from behind the leather sofa. Too short. Too slender.

"It's not him," she said, knowing the silhouette didn't match the man who'd attacked her in the park. She didn't know whether she felt disappointment or relief. While she wanted to catch the stalker and put an end to her fear, confronting whoever was following her was scary, too.

"Don't hurt me." The high-pitched voice came from the shadows.

"He's only a kid," Craig said.

"What are you doing here?" Summer and the boy asked each other at the same time.

"I came to feed the fish. Mark, I mean Mr. Hanson, is in Europe. I take care of the pool, too."

"In the middle of the night?" Craig asked wryly, amusement coloring his tone.

"Hey, man, I just got in from a party." Fish swam to the top of the tank, almost attacking the food. The kid's eyes darted nervously from the fish back to them. "If I'd known you were coming, I would have stopped in earlier." The boy edged around the tank as if he wasn't quite sure if they'd come to rob the place or not, but he was clearly reluctant to take unnecessary chances.

Craig accompanied the boy out, giving him his friend's European address and phone number and telling him to call Mark before the cops. Craig even gave the kid money to make the overseas call.

After the boy left, weariness caught up with Summer. She was so tired she couldn't contain her yawns and stumbled off to a downstairs guest room. The stunning brass bed with white cotton sheets and a luxuriant satin comforter proved irresistible. Sleeping on a different floor from Craig somehow made sharing the house less intimate.

The following day, Craig put his laptop to use, dividing his time between the computer and the phone. Summer took a walk along the beach and catnapped by the pool, resting for the party at Harry's while she tried not to think about how much Craig appealed to her and how much he'd objected to her accepting Harry's invitation. But he'd finally agreed to accompany her.

Throughout the day, Craig spoke on the phone, using his voice like a carver used his hands, shaping wood until he'd created what he desired. He cajoled, he praised, he ordered, and once he even got angry—all without raising his voice. The command in his tone was always there, demanding obedience, yet he spoke with polite consideration and respect.

She found herself not so much listening to the meaning of his words as he bought products overseas, arranged for shipping and distribution, but letting his rhythmic speech soothe her with his strength, his sincerity and candor. That a man who exuded such power could so easily admit several times during the day that he didn't know something, she found not only admirable, but sexy.

Okay, so she liked the guy. More than liked him. She was beginning to care for Craig in a way that was new to her. She considered him a friend and business partner first, but every time she remembered his kiss, excitement zinged through her. The passion added another dimension to her genuine admiration of the man to whom she'd brought so much trouble.

She'd turned his life on end. He hadn't gone to the office to work since the day she'd arrived. He'd gone to bat at court for her. Had paid for Gran's care. Had moved out of his home to hide with her. All without complaint.

She knew that the even temper he showed to the world obscured the depth of his emotions. That he'd loved his first wife deeply was evident in the pictures of her on the walls of his home and the fact he'd remained single. She'd never heard of another man going to the extremes he had to have children. There were millions of single parents struggling to raise their children—but how many of them would have started the task knowing they would be the children's sole support and provider? How many men wanted children so badly they'd go to the trouble and expense of hiring a surrogate to bear them?

Not many. Craig was a rarity among men. The more time she spent with him, the more she appreciated his uncommon qualities.

Although she repeatedly told herself his kiss had meant nothing, he stirred within her burgeoning emotions like caring and concern. And desire. Belatedly, she'd realized with frustration she was setting herself up for another rejection.

Sure, he treated her with courtesy, but he treated strangers and business acquaintances with equal politeness. He hadn't complained about the inconveniences because that wasn't his nature—but silence didn't mean he didn't mind what she'd done to him.

No doubt as soon as the twins were born, and once he became wrapped up in caring for the babies, he'd forget about her. She'd go back to her life—what was left of it. If she was already attached to him after such a short time, how much worse off would she be after seven or eight months?

She dozed fitfully throughout the late afternoon and awakened without feeling refreshed. The skies clouded and a fog rolled in with the rain, isolating the house, leaving her restless and vulnerable. The rain fell irritatingly on the roof, slashing the windows, the droplets blocking the view. She wished they didn't have to go out in the storm.

Although she'd insisted on attending, she couldn't shake an ominous premonition about the party. A leisurely shower didn't change her mind. She might have avoided Harry's party, but most of the people she'd known when she'd worked at his law firm would be there. Craig could eyeball everyone and they'd both ask questions. They couldn't afford to miss an opportunity like this. Besides, Gran would be there and they could visit.

Craig had told Summer to borrow one of Mark Hanson's wife's dresses from the closet since she had nothing appropriate to wear. The plain black cocktail dress was a bit snug in the bust but otherwise fitted perfectly. She spread the wigs out on the bed, deciding which one to wear, wondering which one Craig preferred. Her gaze was drawn to a cascade of platinum, but she skipped over it to her sentimental favorite, the red, waist length wig she'd worn the day she'd first met Craig.

She picked up the red wig but reluctantly set it down. She didn't want to stand out in a crowd. Instead, she placed the more sedate dark auburn wig with straight, shoulder-length strands on her head since it most closely matched the style and color of her own hair, and she'd used this wig while she'd worked for Harry. And since the stalker had found her while she'd worn this wig in the park, he'd easily recognize her, also. Moving to the vanity, she brushed on bold cosmetics, outlining her eyes, dabbing just a hint of color on her cheeks and finishing with a bright and brazen apricot on her lips.

Stepping back, she deemed the dress too drab and conservative for a party and dug into her bag, debating between a costume-jewelry giraffe pin and a bold silver-and-black scarf. With a grin, she draped the scarf around her neck and secured it with the pin.

There. She looked elegant, but not stodgy. Young, but stylish. Most importantly, she looked a helluva lot more confident than she felt. She couldn't decide if her premonition of disaster was simply her way of telling herself Craig was not a real date and nothing romantic would happen between them tonight, or if her changing hormones were simply making her uneasy.

She met Craig in the foyer. He was stunning in a navy sport coat and slacks with a white turtleneck that emphasized his tan.

His perceptive gray eyes took her in and he grinned appreciatively at her dress and hair. "I could go out with you every night and I'd always be curious to see whether you'd show up as a blonde, brunette or redhead. Ready?"

"Yes."

Hoping her nervousness didn't show, she squared her shoulders. She was taking a risk tonight, deliberately exposing herself to the stalker. But she had to find out who was after her or she'd never again feel safe.

"If you spot anyone suspicious, just point him out. You leave the confronting to me, okay?" Craig took an umbrella from the hall closet, opened the front door and urged her into the night.

Brushing her foreboding aside, she ducked into the rain. Craig shielded her from the worst of the weather, and she supposed he'd like to shield her from the stalker, too. While she appreciated his sentiment, and being coddled had some good points, just because she'd admitted her anxiety, she didn't want him treating her as though she was helpless.

Craig opened her door for her, walked around to

the driver's side and hurriedly slid into the car. "Don't forget to buckle up."

"Is all this concern for me or the babies?" she asked. The words had just slipped out. Not thinking ahead was so uncharacteristic of her usual behavior, she figured the pregnancy must be playing havoc with her mood.

Craig didn't seem to notice her distress. Still, she tensed until he chuckled.

After starting the car, he turned on the headlights and the windshield wipers. "Right now, you and the twins are a package deal."

She forced herself to take a deep breath. Anger wilted and bittersweet thoughts took root. Of course he thought her and the twins a package—what else could he think? Although she was honored he valued her as the mother of his children, their date was a sham. His concern for her wouldn't last.

"Actually," he interrupted her thoughts, "I'm more worried about this storm. There'll be accidents in this poor visibility."

She tried not to think about the steep, winding road they'd be taking until they headed inland to Glendale and the fancy restaurant where Harry always held his parties. "We need to get our stories straight for the evening."

"What do you mean?"

"These people know me. I worked for Harry for three years. They're bound to be curious about where I've been and what I've been doing. They'll pump me for information about you."

"Tell them the truth."

She almost choked. Had he guessed at her final

deception? Was that censure she heard in his tone or her imagination working overtime? She remained still, tensed for the guillotine blade to fall, waiting to see what he'd say next, knowing the car ride during a storm where he had to concentrate on his driving was no place for a fight.

"What truth?" she bluffed. "You want me to tell them about the stalker?"

"Tell them we're married. That'll explain your absence, change in job and living quarters. Hopefully, your friends will be so enthralled they won't question your current whereabouts too closely."

He wanted her to play the happy newlywed. He was right that the announcement of her sudden marriage could explain away much of the mystery around her. Of course, they didn't have a real marriage. Never had. The paperwork didn't matter—not when they'd divorce after the children were born.

When she'd signed the papers, she'd never anticipated having to explain her situation to anyone. She didn't expect any of her friends and associates to know she'd even married, never mind divorced. "And the babies?"

"I see no reason to mention the unusual circumstances of your pregnancy."

"Okay. Tonight I'll be Mrs. Summer Banks."

"You don't have to sound so reluctant. It's not as if you'll be lying."

She swallowed a hysterical laugh. If she didn't get herself under control soon, he was going to suspect something was wrong. Thankful the weather forced him to keep his attention on the road, she fidgeted in her seat. Surely if he could have seen her eyes, he might have guessed she hadn't told him the whole truth.

He spoke again, seeming not to notice her momentary inability to speak. "Will posing as my wife be so difficult? Is there a reason you don't want to introduce me to your friends and co-workers?"

"Of course not. I'm a little embarrassed I didn't invite them to our wedding."

"We can tell them we eloped, that we just couldn't resist one another."

At the teasing tone in his voice, she told herself to relax or she'd never get through the evening. Pretending to be his wife shouldn't be difficult if she prepared.

A thick fog slithered along the ground, like a fat gray snake. Ignoring her nerves that tightened with every passing mile, she attempted to distract herself from the ceaseless rain and her uneasiness by concocting details to match their elopement.

"We need to get our stories straight. How did we meet?"

"At my attorney's office?"

Well, at least that part of the story was true—even if he didn't remember her. But then they hadn't been introduced; she'd been working at her desk as he strode by.

"And we'd known each other how long?"

"A few days?" he suggested.

"And we haven't had time for a honeymoon, okay?"

As they drove up to the restaurant's covered area that protected them from the weather, she wished for a moment that their story was all true, wished that circumstances hadn't forced them together and that he wasn't with her only because of the children.

While the valet parked Craig's car, she perused their elegant surroundings. Owned by a friend and client of Harry Pibbs, the restaurant was noted for the multimillion-dollar deals made in the back booths just as much as for the shrimp and chicken over linguini salad and their extra dry martinis.

Almost immediately, Summer spotted Harry in the crowd. She led Craig over to make introductions.

Harry's eyes lit up when he greeted her with a warm smile and seconds later embraced her in a tight hug. "Hi, stranger. You are a sight for this old man's eyes."

"You're not old," she protested truthfully. Harry ran ten miles to work every morning. He played golf on weekends and watched his weight.

Not even Harry's expensive bay rum cologne could cover the scent of the cigars he hid from his wife. As he enveloped her, the familiar scent and the warmth of his greeting brought tears to her eyes. Too much time had passed since she'd seen her friends.

She pulled away gently, a lump in her throat. "Harry Pibbs, meet my husband, Craig Banks."

Harry's eyes crinkled at the corners. He broke into a huge grin and gave her a knowing look. "So that's what happened to you."

Craig and her old boss shook hands. "I'm afraid your loss was my gain."

Within moments, a crowd of former associates engulfed Summer. Someone handed her a drink from a passing waiter and the secretaries plied her with questions. She attempted to look suitably happy and head over heels in love as she explained her elopement and craned her neck to look for Gran.

Instead, she spotted Kendrick, huddled with another man and accompanied by a stunning blonde in a dress so low cut she could have been advertising implant surgery. The blonde had attached herself to Kendrick, but her gaze roved over the men in the crowd.

Summer knew she shouldn't be mean, but Kendrick could do better. The woman might as well have had the word "starlet" tattooed across her ample chest. Kendrick seemed oblivious to the woman, treating the blonde much the way he'd treated Summer, and she considered whether the lack of passion in their relationship had been as much Kendrick's fault as hers. This time, she turned over the idea with a new confidence she'd never had before, a confidence being with Craig had given her.

Before she could think the idea through, she spotted Gran beside the bar talking to Harry and Mabel. Mabel's lips pinched as she scowled at the handsome Fred holding Gran's arm. In contrast to the sour-faced woman, Gran glowed, looking elegant in a sequined gold blouse with a floor-length black skirt. Spotting Summer, Gran, with Fred in tow, broke away from the attorney and his wife.

Summer grinned as Fred hurried to keep up. Obviously, Gran's ankle had recovered.

Her grin faded a bit when Uncle Bob came into view behind Fred. She hadn't expected him to turn up, but then he occasionally threw business Harry's way. She should have anticipated his presence, but with all she had on her mind lately, she could forgive herself for forgetting a few details.

Uncle Bob wore a pleasant expression. With the free booze of an open bar, the man was in his element. As usual, his gray suit was immaculate, his hair neatly trimmed around the bald spot at his crown. He trailed behind Gran and Fred, walking steadily, if a bit deliberately.

Summer enveloped Gran in a hug. Although they'd only been apart a few days, she was accustomed to daily visits. "I've missed you. You look wonderful."

"Freddy's been taking good care of me," Gran praised Fred loudly, then whispered so only Summer could hear, "Harry's telling everyone you're married. Bob is suspicious."

Glad for her grandmother's warning, Summer's thoughts raced. Uncle Bob might be a drunk, but he'd always had a keen intelligence that tonight made her wary. She moved out of Gran's arms and offered a nod of greeting to Fred, all the while hoping Uncle Bob wouldn't trip up the story she and Craig had concocted.

Fred leaned forward and planted a kiss on her cheek. "I hear congratulations are in order. You're a married lady?"

Craig must have seen Uncle Bob heading her way. Her husband smoothly cut through the crowd to her side. Without saying a word, he slipped an arm around her waist and pulled her against him, his look adoring. She only wished his feelings were genuine.

Ah, how she ached for him, yearned for him to want her as much as she wanted him. At the thought, the ragged pulse of her breathing accelerated. All her good intentions of keeping a safe distance from him vanished, leaving her with a yen to tilt her mouth up to his for another searing kiss.

Dreamily, she looked back at Craig as she responded to Fred's question. Uncle Bob arrived just in time to hear her explanation. "Craig and I met at Dean, Atherson, and Jackson. It was love at first sight and we eloped the next day."

Fred's eyes widened. "The next day? But...you barely knew one another."

Uncle Bob chuckled. "Our practical little Summer fell for the oldest line in the book."

Just who did he think he was to question her morality?

"I didn't fall for a line," Summer snapped. "I'm married." Craig seemed content to let her deal with her family, but his hand tightened on her waist, warning her to be careful.

"She picked a fine man." Gran backed Summer up, her words easing the mounting tension. "I couldn't be more pleased with her decision."

Fred turned to her grandmother, his voice both accusatory and surprised. "Why didn't you ever mention Summer eloped?"

At the unexpected question, Summer's pulse rate skyrocketed. She didn't know what to say. Of course it would have been natural for Gran to have told Fred that she'd married. The omission was suspicious.

Gran's brow wrinkled. "I thought I told you. I'm quite sure I did."

Good old Gran had come through once again. She suppressed a smile at her grandmother's outfoxing

Fred with a pretense of senility to slouch off the awkward question.

Fred frowned, then shrugged. "May I see your ring?"

Acid churned in her stomach and Summer thought fast. "It's at the jeweler's. One of the settings loosened yesterday. Thank goodness I didn't lose a stone."

Fred nodded, his face instantly serious. "Next time you visit your grandmother, I'd like to see what you picked out. I'm thinking of popping the question to my girlfriend."

Gran squealed. "How exciting. I hope I won't be losing you."

"Never fear. I like the work at Jarrod's."

"How's Kendrick taking your new status?" Uncle Bob asked Summer, a sly look in his eyes. The acid in her stomach rose another notch.

"Why don't you go ask him?" Craig suggested, his tone soft yet defiantly menacing.

Gran laughed. Summer bit back another grin. She couldn't remember when her grandmother had last had this good a time.

A band warmed up and the loud music made talking difficult. The lights dimmed. Fred asked Gran to dance and the two of them hit the parquet floor like Astaire and Rogers. Uncle Bob wandered off with a scowl, leaving her and Craig alone.

Craig handed his glass to a passing waiter. "Would you like to dance?" he asked Summer.

"I'm out of practice. I'll probably step all over your feet."

"I'll take my chances." Craig gathered her into his

arms and her body responded before her mind could drum up another protest. She immediately forgot about the steps and concentrated on how good his hand felt in hers.

"Aren't you holding me a little too close?" she asked, striving to put more distance between them.

He chuckled. "Newly married couples do that. You dance beautifully." His voice thickened with approval. "That comeback you made to Fred about the ring was exceptional."

"My claim to fame," she teased, pleased by his compliment. "I'm a very good liar."

"Remind me to buy you a ring and make an honest woman out of you."

She stumbled. "That's not necessary."

"I think it is."

She knew he wasn't proposing but merely wanted to keep up the appearance of a conventional marriage. After she delivered the babies, she'd return the ring.

He was a smooth, confident dancer and she had no trouble following his lead. With one hand on the small of her back, he shot heat straight through her dress. She inhaled his clean scent, surprised his breath smelled of mint and not alcohol.

His arms tightened around her. His tone was husky in her ear. "If everyone believes we're married, then the stalker might realize you're under my protection and back off."

Disappointment flowed through her at the reminder. Every move he made was for the children. She should know that by now. No doubt he was dancing with her, holding her close, in hopes the stalker was in the room. He was signaling that she was his, marking his territory in a way as old as time.

And she didn't mind one bit.

She liked the idea of his protecting her. She liked the cherishing look in his eyes, the sensation of his solid shoulder under her hand, the way his arms made her feel safe. Warm. Contented.

It's not real.

So what?

For once, she put her practical side behind. She'd pretend this was a normal evening out for a real husband and wife. What could be the harm?

Protected in Craig's arms, she dreamily laid her head against his chest. His footsteps slowed until they were barely moving, just swaying together on the dance floor.

His hand, naughtily suggestive, swirled sensual circles on her arm. With each breath, she grew more relaxed and she couldn't contain a sigh of unmistakable pleasure. Desire coursed through her, strong and hard. She wanted him to kiss her, wanted him to sweep her into his arms, carry her off to bed. She wanted to know what it was like to make love with a man who respected her. She wanted to see what would happen to all the emotions that swirled inside, making her first icy hot, then steaming cold.

Backing away would be prudent. Following through on her blossoming desires would be a mistake. Her common sense argued for restraint, but when his mouth brushed her forehead and cheek, she wanted to give in to the need to discover if Craig was different enough to sustain this wonderful, floating excitement. She didn't know what was happening to her, but she didn't want this moment to end.

The music concluded, and Craig drew away with a smile so devastating her body temperature rose a degree. His gaze met hers straight on and stunned her as if someone had stolen the air right out of her lungs. With some effort, she resisted the urge to throw herself back into his arms.

Forcing her eyes away, she watched Gran and Fred approach. In a romantic daze, she and Gran switched partners.

She was dancing with Fred, who was probably a much better dancer than Craig—but the magic was gone. Chemistry was such a strange thing. Briefly, she wondered what caused her to be so attracted to Craig but to feel nothing but brotherly affection for Fred, who was kind and just as attractive in his own way.

"I know you hate it when Kendrick and Bob fight," Fred told her. "You needn't worry about your uncle Bob. He hasn't gone near Kendrick."

"Thanks. You've been a good friend to Gran and me."

Dancing with Fred was comfortable. They'd known each other since they were kids. Perhaps he was too familiar to ever be exciting.

But what had gone wrong between her and Kendrick? Different values, different commitments to what each found important? Perhaps she'd never know.

"I wish I could do more," Fred told her. "Your grandmother seems lonely when you don't visit as often."

Guilt pricked at her. "I've been busy." She knew the excuse was lame.

"Hey, you just got married. Don't worry. I look in on her often."

"Thanks, I don't know what—"

A hand landed on her shoulder and she jumped. Kendrick stood beside her. "Can I cut in?"

Fred looked at her, leaving the decision to her. She nodded and Kendrick took over. From across the dance floor, she could see Craig stiffen. Was he jealous?

She wished.

"So how is the movie going?" she asked in the awkward silence.

"Fine. How's married life?"

"Fine." Had the conversations between them always been so stilted?

"You didn't mention it at the bowling alley. How come?" he demanded.

"I don't know. It was just kind of new and special and I wanted to keep it to myself," she prevaricated, wishing for Gran to save her again.

"Kind of like how I want to keep my story to myself until it's written," he muttered understandingly. He drew back and gave her a hard look. "You've never been secretive before. What's going on?"

Before she could answer, the room was plunged into darkness. The band stopped playing. Someone screamed. There were several nervous titters.

"Damn. Lightning must have knocked out the power. Stay here, I'll be right back."

Summer didn't move. She didn't want Kendrick to leave her alone in the darkness. Breathing deeply and telling herself nothing bad could happen in a room full of people, she tried to calm her jittery nerves.

A hand clamped over her mouth. The scarf around her neck tightened.

Terror shot strength into her limbs. A harsh, rasping sob escaped her lips. She twisted, digging her elbow behind her, but striking only air. She raised her hands to try to free the constriction around her throat. The scarf drew tighter, yanking her off balance and against her attacker. Her eyes teared. Her lungs burned.

A husky voice whispered, "Get rid of him. Get rid of all of them."

Chapter Eight

The instant the lights flickered on, Craig searched for Summer amid the elegant crowd. Thinking of her, worrying about her safety, had become a habit. Apparently a necessary one. He glimpsed her across the room, bent over and coughing, then a crowd of onlookers closed in around her, cutting her off from his sight. Idiots! Why didn't they help? Every nerve in his body suddenly crackled with impatience. He had to reach her.

"Out of my way." He shouldered past groups of gawkers, keeping Summer in sight. At first, she appeared to be choking. He prayed a sip of soda had gone down the wrong pipe and that she'd straighten and signal that she'd recovered.

When she didn't, sweat broke out on his brow and trickled down his cheek. He wanted to shout, knock over people to reach her.

Keep cool. She'll be all right. She has to be all right.

The murmuring crowd parted to let him through, and as he neared, the painful, hacking gasps Summer emitted grew worse. As if fighting pain, she curled her hands into claws.

God, no. Please don't let her be poisoned. Don't let her die.

He wouldn't fail another woman. Never again.

Clearly on the verge of collapse, Summer swayed on her feet. Finally, he reached her side. Horrified by her raspy fight for air, he scooped her into his arms. With large, purposeful strides, he forced the crowd to scatter from his path.

This time, he'd make it to the hospital. This time, he wouldn't be too late.

Glancing down, he noted the chalk white color of her face, sweat beading on her brow, her clammy hand clutching his neck. Her whole body spasmed with each breath and unnerved him.

His heart pumped panic into his chest. Afraid there might not be time to reach the hospital, he searched the crowd for help, spied Harry by the front door and ordered, "Call 911."

Summer shook her head violently. Her voice was a mere croak.

"What is it?" He lowered his ear near her lips. "Tell me again."

Summer lifted her head. "Home."

As if the one word had taken all her effort, she fell back limp in his arms. At least she'd ceased the awful wheezing. With each ragged breath, color slowly returned to her ashen cheeks and lips. Her auburn wig was mussed, her eyes huge and frightened. Her coughing had stopped. So had the raspy sound that had previously accompanied each lungful of air.

She was going to be okay. So were the babies.

His panic slowly subsided, the tension easing from his neck and shoulders. That his first thoughts had been for Summer and not the babies no longer surprised him. The babies, as much as he loved them, weren't as tangible as the woman whose perfume taunted his senses, whose skin felt softer than cashmere, whose vivid green eyes flashed a silent message he wished he could read without her straining her vocal cords.

"Water," she whispered.

"No problem." He set her in a plush chair by the entryway, motioned a waiter over and asked for a glass of ice water. Returning to her side, Craig held the drink to her lips. "Just sip."

Harry offered his cell phone to Craig. "I dialed 911 and gave our address. Emergency Medical Services needs additional information."

Summer took the glass from Craig, straightened in her seat and gestured for him to give her the phone.

Her scarf was askew. Angry red marks stood out against the whiteness of her throat. Damn it to hell! Someone had tried to strangle her.

Harry and Craig exchanged long glances over her head. The concern in her former boss's eyes could have been faked, but Craig didn't think so. While Craig hesitated a split instant, she grabbed the phone. And Harry rejoined his guests, ushering them back into the main room.

Visibly mustering her strength, she spoke almost normally, albeit with a husky catch, into the receiver. "I'm fine. I choked."

Why was she misleading the emergency operator? The marks on her neck indicated an appetizer hadn't stuck in her windpipe. When the lights had gone out, someone had hurt her. But who?

Craig searched the room. Kendrick had disappeared. Craig couldn't find Gran or Fred, either. They must still be unaware of Summer's problem or they'd be at her side.

"I'm okay now," Summer insisted into the phone. "Don't send an ambulance. Sorry to have troubled you."

Troubled you? The attack could have been fatal.

It had been his responsibility to protect her, and he'd failed. Right now, his first concern was Summer's immediate safety. Leaving became a priority as there were too many people here for him to protect her properly. He should never have left her side.

"I'm sorry," he told her.

"For what?"

"For not being there when you needed me."

Her brilliant eyes bored into him. "I'm usually very capable of taking care of myself."

"That's probably the reason you're still alive," he muttered grimly.

Harry had returned silently and overheard Craig's last comment. His eyes darted from side to side. After he seemingly assured himself no one would hear, he lowered his voice. "Summer, come see me. Soon. There's something you need to know." Before either of them could ask questions, Harry departed, drawing the few remaining guests back into the main room. "Show's over, folks. She's going to be fine."

Craig frowned at the man's mysterious words and wished he could go after him and make him explain, but getting Summer to safety took precedence. As people returned to the party and the band struck up another tune, Craig knelt by her side and spoke in a low tone so only she could hear. "Do you want to call the police?"

"They'd ask where we live. I don't want to lie and I don't want to give them our new address. Besides—" her hand moved to her neck "—I didn't see who did this."

Knowing her arguments made sense, he reluctantly agreed. Damn it. How could he protect her from this maniac? How could he stop someone he couldn't even recognize?

Craig gave her no choice about leaving right away. Coming out of hiding had been a mistake. One he didn't intend to repeat. Their situation demanded they slink back into seclusion. The sooner they crawled into their hidey-hole, the better he could protect her. Besides, he hadn't gained any new information at the party—and the risk of staying was too great.

He'd almost lost Summer and his unborn children. The realization nearly paralyzed him. His feelings for her had grown and deepened. For too long, he'd kept his heart free from impossible yearnings. But now, roiling emotions simmered beneath the surface of his worried thoughts as if waiting for the chance to break free of his control. Only the urgent perception she was still exposed to danger goaded him into action.

When Summer's grandmother and Fred finally approached, he welcomed their company. He could safely leave Summer long enough to have the car brought around front. Despite her despair and the longing to comfort her grandmother he felt in Summer's soul, when the car arrived, he allowed Summer only one hug from Gran, then hurried her away.

They departed into the stormy night that he hoped to use to his advantage. Before he pulled onto the freeway, he turned numerous times, doubling back until he was positive no one was following.

As vulnerable and shaken as Summer was, she questioned his evasive tactics. "Is someone after us?"

"I'm not sure." He glanced at her, reached over and squeezed her hand. "If they were, I've surely lost them by now. Are you up to telling me exactly what happened?"

She kept hold of his hand. "There's not much to tell. The lights went out. Someone grabbed my scarf and choked me. I couldn't see a thing."

She was holding back, but out of reluctance to spill the details, or from the fear of reliving a horrifying incident, he wasn't sure. "How did you get away?"

"Even before the lights came back on, he let me go."

Her words confirmed his suspicion. The stalker's intent was not murder. Somehow that didn't make him feel better. "Why did he let you go?"

"I don't know."

"Did someone or something scare him off?"

She tucked a strand of the wig behind her ear. "I could only think about drawing air into my lungs. I almost blacked out."

At the telling strain in her tone, he cursed himself for putting her through an interrogation. But, he needed a lead. She'd given him nothing to go on.

"Maybe he was afraid the lights would come on, and he'd be caught in the act."

"No. I think he intended to release me. Right before he let go of his stranglehold on my scarf, he whispered a threat. He said, 'Get rid of him. Get rid of all of them.'"

A chill stroked his back and froze the marrow of his bones. "The *him* has to be me."

"Or the words could have been the ranting of a crazy person."

"Perhaps." He remained unconvinced. "Anyone who resorts to stalking is unbalanced. I'd hoped the stalker might back off after seeing us attend the party together. Most stalkers are bullies. With me around protecting you, I'd hoped he might give up. Obviously, I was wrong." He frowned and looked over at her. She was shivering, and he turned up the heat. "I'll have you warm in a minute."

"I don't think I'll ever be warm again."

He slanted a glance at her. "When I kissed you, you were plenty warm."

"You think a kiss will make me all better?" she snapped.

"All better—no. But better—yes."

At his words, she sagged in her seat. He held her hand tight. If taking her mind off her problems with a kiss could help lessen the relentless load, he'd stop the car and take her into his arms.

She looked so defenseless that he ached to hold her, vowing to do so at the first opportunity. Meanwhile, he wouldn't keep his thoughts to himself. Summer had said she didn't want to be sheltered from his suspicions. Her tenacity would see her through.

He voiced the fear that had haunted him ever since she'd repeated her attacker's threat. "Do you think get 'rid of all of them' referred to me *and* the twins?"

"Yes," she replied without hesitation. "Do you hate me for putting your children in danger?"

"I could never hate you."

His words, meant to reassure her, seemed to have the opposite effect. She tensed, drawing her hand from his as if she'd been burned.

"What are you thinking?" he asked quietly, non-threateningly.

"Nothing."

"Tell me. Please."

She sighed. "Love and hate are supposed to be two sides of the same coin. One feeling isn't supposed to exist without the possibility of the other. Yet the only strong feelings I seem to inspire are ones that cause a crazy man to stalk me. I was thinking that I've forgotten what normal life is like. I was wallowing in self-pity. Now aren't you sorry you asked?" she said in a that-will-teach-you-not-to-pry-into-my-thoughts tone.

"Could you hate your grandmother?" he countered.

"Of course not!"

"Then you don't love her?"

"Of course I... Yes, I see your point."

"Oh, I'm not done with you yet." She braced as if for a fight. All in all, her stiff posture was preferable to her sagging limply against the seat. Deciding he was on the right track, he kept up the pressure. "What makes you think you don't inspire strong feelings?"

Her voice went flat. "I'm not going there."

"Where?"

"Into my past relationship with Kendrick. It doesn't matter. It's not relevant. It's none of your damn business."

"I'm making your past my business. I'm making *you* my business. That man is a complete egotist. Just because things didn't work out with him doesn't mean you can't find another man to love."

She turned to him. "Are you volunteering to take me to bed."

"Yes."

"Why?"

If she had to ask, she had no idea how much he ached to touch her and comfort her, to taste every inch of her, to give her pleasure.

"How do I know I'm not just a convenience for you?" she asked. "You can't date other women right now. Maybe you're turning to me out of a purely physical need."

Her words hurt, but she spoke from inexperience, and he cautioned himself to patience. "Is that what you think? Didn't you feel what I did when we kissed? When we danced? Do you think the intensity of feelings like ours happens often?"

When he glanced at her, she averted her gaze. Clearly, she found looking at him too painful. Her hands twisted in her lap. "I don't know."

"Well, I do."

She remained silent during the rest of the ride to Malibu, apparently giving his suggestion some consideration. Powerful anticipation kept him wide awake as he drove. Would she take him up on his offer? Was she thinking about what he'd said or thinking up another excuse to deny herself what he could give her? What she could give him?

He stopped only once, at an all-night grocery store to pick up supplies. Fifteen minutes later, he pulled into the driveway. Setting the scene of seduction filled his thoughts, though he grimaced wryly when his first move was to look right and left at the neighbors' yards and across the street to see if anyone followed.

The narrow street remained empty and dark. He circled to the passenger side to help her from the car. Summer met him halfway, and he held the umbrella over them and the groceries as protection against the driving rain.

"This is a good night for hot cocoa and snuggling under a blanket in front of a fire," she murmured.

At the comfy scene she'd suggested—especially the part about cuddling in front of a fire that indicated her thoughts had been running along the same romantic lines as his—gladness filled his heart. "I'll see what I can do about the fire. Why don't you put the food away, maybe make some cocoa."

After he locked the door behind them, they slipped off their wet shoes. He padded to the fireplace where a stack of oak already waited in a metal grate. One strike of a match set the center log burning. The paper kindling around the store-bought wood caught quickly, and barely ten minutes passed before the oak blazed and took the chill from the room.

He appraised the giant floor-to-ceiling windows next. In daylight, the view of the Pacific was the house's best feature; at night, the black glass seemed cold against the endless rain. After he closed the blinds, the room seemed cheerier, cozier.

He walked past the living-room bar to a stereo system and popped in several CDs. What else? The lady had asked to cuddle. Where better than with blankets and pillows by the fire? He vaulted the stairs, returned with an armful of bedding and arranged a comfortable nook near the fireplace.

He didn't dim the lights, and several minutes later, she returned with two cups of cocoa. He wasn't sorry the lights were still bright. Not when he saw the tightness in her dark emerald eyes and the determined set of her lips as if she'd have to endure his seduction.

He sat on the floor, then leaned back against a pillow in front of the fire. "Now this is better than some stuffy party." He patted the pillow next to him. "Come have a seat."

She clenched her jaw until a muscle throbbed in her neck. Still, she did as he asked, handing him the cocoa, which he set down beside him, then sliding under the blanket next to him, close, but not touching.

Casually, he slipped an arm across her shoulder. When he reached with his free hand for the cocoa instead of her, she relaxed, but only a smidgen. "You found marshmallows." She didn't answer. Apparently, he'd have to be more direct. "I won't attack you like some sex-starved kid. I won't do anything you don't want me to."

"I know." She set her cup down on the floor and twisted her hands in the blanket. "It's just that—"

"You needn't explain. Once I start touching you, I'll stop when you ask. You can change your mind. Do you understand what I'm saying? If I kiss you, it can be a good-night kiss, the first of many kisses, or kisses that lead to taking off your clothes."

His assurances drew the first smile he'd received from her since the attack that night and warmed his insides. Her eyes sparkled with unshed tears. "I don't want to disappoint you."

"That will depend..."

"On what?"

"On whether you're ever going to kiss me."

She rubbed her brow, looking cute and confused at the same time. "I've already kissed you."

"*I* initiated the kiss. *You* haven't kissed *me*."

"I see."

"I don't think you do. Do you know how hard making the first move is for a man? If you'd rejected me, I might not have worked up my courage to try again...for, oh, at least an hour or two."

She chuckled again, and he adored the deep, throaty sound hovering in the air between them and beckoning like a Siren's call. More importantly, she'd relaxed against him. But relaxed wasn't what he had in mind for Summer Warren, no, Summer Banks, he corrected, reminding himself she was his legal wife.

"Women have this love business easy," he continued. "Men have to plan the seduction, guess at the timing, the words, the movements. Men have to risk rejection. Women only have to decide yes or no."

"That's not easy, either. Men can so easily separate the act of making love from their emotions."

"Plenty of men walk around with broken hearts, too."

"I know. If I don't take chances, I may never win the pot of gold at the end of the rainbow."

He cupped her chin, resting his thumb on the pulse in her neck. "Love isn't won. Love is a journey. Love is deciding you want to spend your life with someone. Love is a feeling that comes from inside and enriches what you see, say and do. Love is a part of you that you nourish because it's special and rare.''

"How do you know when you've found it?" she asked, her voice low, husky.

He released her chin and dropped his hand to his knee. "You won't have to ask because you'll know."

She tilted her head, considering his words. For a moment, his heart skipped a beat when he thought she might stand up and leave.

But apparently, she'd made up her mind to stay. As if fearing she might back away if she didn't fully commit herself, she scooted over until she'd draped herself across his lap, going from innocent to vamp. The little minx. What was she up to?

Her eyes twinkled, brimming with unshed emotions. "Don't be afraid. I'm going to kiss you now."

He needed every ounce of concentration to hold perfectly still as she ran her hands through his hair, across his brow, over his lips to the pulse at his neck, all the while staring deep into his eyes.

Idly, he smoothed back her hair—her wig, he amended—and he wondered if she'd trust him enough tonight to reveal more of her secrets, perhaps her real hair color. But she didn't show much interest in conversation.

She tugged his head down. Her lips nibbled his, firing his blood, his imagination, his hopes. Wrapping his arms around her, he encouraged her to find her own pace, realizing what a difficult task he'd set himself.

He longed to run his hands along her spine, inch

down the long zipper of her dress and expose the soft skin of her back. But he sensed she was not yet ready. He ached to tug the dress from her shoulders and reveal her full breasts. Most of all, he wanted her to trust him enough to tear down her defensive walls. He wasn't after a physical conquest, but a spiritual fusion. He wanted her trust.

She deepened their kiss. Together, they slid onto the pillows, the hot cocoa all but forgotten except for the lingering sweet taste of marshmallows on her lips. He lay on his back, she on top of him, controlling their tempo.

Her kiss sent singing heat directly to his groin. Forgetting his vow, he reached for the zipper of her dress.

"Not yet," she murmured, gently braceleting his wrists and placing them above his shoulders.

He laced his fingers tightly together behind his head and urged her to have her way. Straddling him, she unbuttoned his shirt, slowly, sensuously, exploring the ridges of his chest muscles and the hollows of his stomach.

Her tongue swirled over a nipple, and when he didn't react to her taunt, she nipped him lightly. He flinched, unable to control his ragged breathing. He thought she'd next draw down his zipper. She surprised him by rising gracefully to her feet.

"Don't move," she ordered, a wicked gleam in her eyes. "It's getting warm in here."

"You're definitely heating up the room," he agreed, wishing she'd hurry and do whatever she intended—preferably take off her clothes and return to him. But she was in no hurry to end his suspense.

She had him partially sit up, then she bent over to

place a pillow behind his head before easing him back down. Leaving him in a comfortable position to watch her, she stepped back and ran her tongue over her lips. With slim fingers, she untied her scarf, removed the giraffe pin and tossed the wisp of silk onto his chest.

Her feminine scent wafted up from the garment, heightening his desire. Holding still proved impossible. He started to sit up and gather her back.

She stalled him by turning around, kneeling and lifting her hair. "Could you please help?"

He wanted to take his time, but she was killing him with her slowness. His shaking hands managed the job somewhat clumsily. Just as he finished unzipping her dress and reached to tug it from her shoulders, she leaned away and escaped his reach. For a moment, he thought she might flee. With her back still to him, she shimmied out of the dress, leaving a pool of black crepe at her feet.

He sucked in air. Beneath the dress, she wore a black bra, matching panties and dark stockings with garters, perfect foils for her firm, creamy curves. She strode to the fireplace, hips swaying enticingly, and his mouth went dry.

Raising one knee and propping her foot on the stack of logs, she slowly rolled down one stocking, then the other, prolonging the act as if she knew exactly how she made his pulse race.

"Summer?"

"Hmm?" She glanced over her shoulder at him, a saucy look on her face.

"I lied when I said I could stop at any time. If you

remove one more article of clothing, I won't be able to account for my actions.''

Her bottom lip jutted into an adorable pout. Her gaze wandered to the bulge in his trousers, then back to his face. She swallowed hard.

"Are you trying to hurry me?" she asked.

Suddenly, he knew everything was going to be all right. She might tease him unmercifully, but she intended to feed his raging fire.

"Around you, I don't have as much willpower as I thought."

She chuckled at his admission. "In that case, I suggest you take those pants off while I dim the lights."

A moment later, she joined him under the blankets. She hadn't just dimmed the lights, she'd turned them completely off. He could see her only by the flicker of firelight, and although he found the intimate darkness sexy, he felt her tensing.

"Let's take this slow and easy," he whispered into her ear. "Tell me what you like."

"Kiss me."

"Anything to please a lady."

He claimed her lips, not hard and demanding as he wanted, but soft and coaxing in an attempt to delight her.

During the kiss, he slipped off her underwear. Modestly, she kept the blanket up, but she never broke the kiss, never stopped kissing him, never stopped running her hands over his neck and shoulders and back, driving him wild.

He lazily caressed her thighs, his hand drifting down between them. When she stiffened, he pulled back, guessing he was moving too fast.

Slow down, boy.

He broke their kiss and traced a path of kisses down her neck, tasted the dip at her shoulder, outlined the delicate line of her collarbone. All his usual logic deserted him, and he relied on instinct, judging when she wanted more, when to hold back. Common sense told him she had *made love* but had never been *made love to* before. The difference was subtle. The difference was everything that mattered.

If he had any sense at all, he'd pull back now and leave her wanting more, leave her thinking how delicious their intimacies had been until now. But around Summer, keeping his senses proved next to impossible.

Her breasts spilled into his hands and the softest of caresses brought a delicate moan to her lips. When he took first one nipple into his mouth then the other, she whimpered.

Aware of her building restlessness, he nuzzled a path from her breasts to her still-flat stomach. She reached down and tugged his hair. He'd gone far enough. For now.

Teasingly, he floated his fingers over her. This time, her thighs parted to welcome his touch, and he found her slick, heated, ready. Biting back the rising urgency to be inside her, he kissed her mouth again, letting her know how much he wanted her.

Finally, he couldn't hold back for even the space of another breath. Lifting his hips, he centered her beneath him. Entering her slowly an inch at a time was sweet torture.

"You feel wonderful." Her welcoming warmth had him frantic with need. Fighting for control, he withdrew slowly, waiting for her to raise her hips and meet his return.

Instinctively, she understood his silent question. Her hips danced, matching his move for move. Tiny groans came from the back of her throat. She clutched his back, wound her long legs around him and urged him on.

Her wild, uninhibited movement stoked the heat until he could barely contain the mounting pressure. He could hold back no more.

"Come with me, Summer."

He reached down between their bodies to help her over the edge, but she shifted away. Her movement was his undoing and he exploded, clutching her shoulders and murmuring her name.

As his heartbeat slowed, she remained silent. Too silent. He gathered her close, sorry she hadn't been able to trust him enough to let go. Maybe next time. He intended to make the next time happen quite soon.

At least he thought she'd enjoyed herself. He snuggled against her, reveling in her feminine scent, in the softness of her skin, in the sound of her panting as her breathing returned to normal.

He caressed her arm, running his fingertips from elbow to shoulder. "Give me a few minutes and then we'll—"

"I don't think so."

The flatness in her tone chilled him. "Tell me what's wrong."

Summer wrapped herself tightly in the blanket. "I don't want to talk."

Now what? She had him completely puzzled. As stiff as a virgin, she averted her eyes from his face, staring into the fire as if she wished he didn't exist. No way would he let her shut him out. "Am I supposed to guess what upset you?"

"Talking makes me feel worse."

"Then let me hold you." He reached for her, but she lay so rigidly, her body language said as clear as any words that she rejected his touch.

What had he done to turn her from warm, welcoming and willing to cold and remote? He hadn't forced her. She'd been eager, her body fully aroused. He didn't understand. He sensed that if he let her shut him out now, she'd close up on him for good.

She meant too much to him to let that happen. Leaving her the blanket, he rolled back on top of her, supported his weight on his elbows and looked directly into her eyes. He wished he could see better. Was that pain he saw on her face? Her cheek glinted and he kissed away a salty, silent tear.

"What's wrong?" he asked again.

She sniffled. "It's just the hormones. Gran told me when she was pregnant with my mother, she often found herself crying for no reason."

He didn't buy her story. "I don't believe you."

He had her trapped, but with the blanket between them, she should feel safe enough from his pressing himself on her again—if that's what bothered her. Somehow he didn't think she feared him.

The fire crackled and the wood popped while he waited for her to say something. Anything. She remained silent. He'd never run up against a wall like this.

"When we made love, did I do something to offend you?" he asked.

"You were wonderful. The problem isn't you."

At least she'd answered. "Making love with you was wonderful. In fact, I'd like to do it again—"

"You aren't going to drop your embarrassing questions, are you? You'll chisel away until your curiosity is satisfied."

"Talk to me. I can't help when I don't understand what's wrong."

"What's wrong is me."

"You?"

"I never respond like I should. If we keep making love, you'll begin to feel cheated."

"Because it wasn't as good for you as you'd hoped?"

She nodded.

Craig swore savagely under his breath. Kendrick, that bastard, must have put these ridiculous notions in her head, and she'd been inexperienced enough to believe him. However, getting mad at Kendrick wouldn't help Summer.

Shoving his anger to the back of his mind, he forced himself to transmit a calm he didn't feel. He rolled off her and clasped his hands behind his head. How could he make her understand?

"Someone is stalking you. In addition, you almost died tonight. You're pregnant. To top it off, this *is* the first time we've made love. I don't know about you, but I certainly was nervous. If stars didn't burst in your head and this wasn't the most fantastic experience of your life, that's understandable under these stressful circumstances."

"The circumstances don't matter. I've never..."

"So what?"

She turned on her side, facing him for the first time. "What do you mean, so what?"

He could bring up how close she'd come or the little matter of her shifting away from his hand at the last moment—but he didn't. He'd heard the anger in her voice and mentally smiled. Rage was better than the icy calm she'd tried to convey. He wanted her fighting for what she wanted, not giving up and withdrawing into silence.

"Did you enjoy making love?"

Raindrops found their way down the chimney and hissed and sizzled as they struck the flames. She was silent so long he didn't think she'd answer. The fire highlighted her cheekbones, but he couldn't read her shadowed eyes.

She laid her hand on his chest, the first time she'd touched him since she'd gone so quiet. "I did enjoy making love."

Unable to resist a grin at her words, he was grateful for the darkness. "Good. Practice makes perfect, you know. Can we do it again?"

She arched her brows. "I'm kind of worn-out."

As much as he wanted another chance to make love, recalling what she'd been through tonight, he didn't press her. This time when he reached for her, she came to him easily, snuggling against his side.

He held her all night. When she wakened in the morning, he realized that he still didn't know her real hair color. She'd remained hidden beneath her blanket, the wig still on.

Suddenly, her hair color didn't seem so important. The rain had stopped. They had an entire day ahead of them. And the stalker didn't know their new location.

With time, he thought they could work out their difficulties. With time, she might grow to love him.

WHILE CRAIG TYPED away on his computer, Summer was grateful for the fax modem that allowed him to keep in touch with his office and suppliers from any phone line. Since she'd messed up every other aspect of his life, she'd hate to ruin his business, too.

While she set the table for breakfast, her thoughts returned to last night. Craig had been so sweet. He'd certainly given her a lot to think about. Her head spun with new thoughts, even hope for her future. If only they could discover the stalker before he found her again, she might find peace—maybe even love.

She found aqua place mats in a kitchen drawer, cereal in the cupboards, and was grateful they'd stopped for groceries on the way back last night. Reaching for her orange juice on the kitchen table, she knocked her purse to the floor. Craig stopped typing and bent over.

God, no. Don't let him see it.

Her wallet spilled open. Several credit cards and her driver's license fell out.

Her heart battered her ribs.

Don't read.

Look at the picture.

Don't read.

While she held her breath in dread, he glanced at the picture on her license. She'd worn her hair short and dark back then. More important than the color of her hair was the placement of his thumb over her last name.

Surreptitiously, she scooped the damning credit cards back into her wallet. Now to retrieve her license.

"Come on. Hand it over. Why do you need to look at a picture when you have the real thing?" she teased, attempting to keep her tone light.

"I've always thought women with dark hair possessed exotic attributes. Now I know it's true. I like your hair dark."

Damn it. She needed the license, and he didn't seem inclined to give it up. Her nerves stretched taut. Keep the conversation light, she reminded herself. "Seems to me you like redheads and blondes, as well."

He looked down at the license. "My favorite..."

His thumb moved. He stared at the license. His eyes narrowed. He frowned.

Fear scrambled down her neck, trampled over her spine and twisted in her stomach.

He knew.

His hand trembled. He dropped the license. His fingers closed into a fist. One look at the rage in his gaze, the hard set of his jaw, and she took a step back.

"You lied to me."

"Yes."

"Your name isn't Warren, is it?"

"No."

She bit her inside cheek, despising herself for her sudden fear. If he put everything together, and he would, she couldn't blame him if he struck her after what she had done. The power she now held over him would break a stronger man.

He lowered his voice to a menacing hiss. "The name Warren is the name on our marriage license."

"Yes."

"You married me using a fake name?"

"Yes."

His voice turned flat, cold. "And exactly what are the legal ramifications of your lie?"

Oh, God. She didn't want to tell him the rest. Couldn't face the affection he'd shown her changing to loathing. But clearly he'd already guessed most of the truth.

She chewed her bottom lip nervously. "According to California law, our marriage isn't valid."

Chapter Nine

"What the hell do you mean our marriage isn't valid?" Craig's voice was all the more deadly for his level tone.

With the blinds drawn back, bright daylight poured into the kitchen. Highlighted by the sun streaming through the windows, she edged away from him. Face shadowed, he stood a few feet away, his back to the ocean.

The reality of what she'd done suddenly hit her with blinding force. She'd made love to a man who didn't even know her real name. She'd lied to him, almost gotten him killed. She had to be demented to think he'd believe her intentions were honorable and forgive her.

She braced to defend herself. He didn't move.

Even though he imagined the worst, she had no reason to be ashamed. She'd used a fake name to protect the babies. "Deliberately lying about my name invalidates our marriage contract," she admitted, wishing he hadn't seen her license, wishing she needn't explain.

Too late for wishing now. Too much was riding on

their relationship not to untangle the lies knotted amid the truth.

Anger, hurt and frustration warred on his face. Beneath roiling emotions, she sensed him harden against her, as if he'd built a concrete wall between them.

"Your real name is Summer Roberts?"

"Yes."

Before she could defend herself, his questions shot at her with the speed of bullets.

"You *are* pregnant?"

Heat rose to her cheeks, but she kept her voice even. "Yes."

"With *my* children?"

She flinched. "Yes, your children. I never had any intention—"

"I don't give a damn about your intentions." He loomed over her, his face inches from hers.

"But—"

"You lied from the beginning. You used me. You placed my children in danger."

"Not intentionally."

He swatted her words aside like flies. "You asked me to protect you. Now you can legally leave and take the babies, too."

His eyes bored into her, his relentless accusations making it difficult to get a word in. Still, she tried. "I wouldn't—"

"Damn right, you won't." He smacked his fist into his palm. "Because if you try, I'll follow you. I'll hunt you down. You won't have one peaceful moment until you give me back my children."

At the menace in his threat, Summer's knees buckled—not from fear at what he might do to her, but from the sheer horror of what he thought her capable of. By God, they'd just made love. He'd spoken to her so tenderly. Now he acted as if she was lower than pond scum.

Sagging against the cold granite counter, she slumped on the floor. She pulled her knees to her chest and her hands to her face and sat rocking. To him, she had done the unforgivable because she'd taken away solid legal control.

How could she have foreseen the future? That Craig had turned out to be a wonderful man was an unexpected bonus. And irrelevant to their contract. The legal trappings didn't motivate her. She'd always intended to give him his children.

On the other hand, legal ties to a stranger were unnecessary. Suppose he'd changed his mind about giving her a divorce? In addition to her other problems, putting herself in the middle of a legal battle she couldn't afford was foolhardy.

Everything had seemed so clear and simple a few months ago. Now, not only had she made a mess of her life, she'd ruined his, too.

"Does Harry Pibbs know you married me under false pretenses?" Craig asked, his eyes narrowed with suspicion. "Is that what he wants to talk to you about?"

Without looking into his angry eyes, she shook her head. "I never discussed my plans with anyone except Gran."

"She approved your shenanigans?"

"Gran thought I should marry you."

"She was right." Craig sighed. "Well, at least

that's one mistake we can fix. Go dress in something appropriate to wear to court.''

Was he hauling her back to the judge? Refusing to be responsible for her since she wasn't really his wife? Surely he wouldn't send her to jail.

Acid burned through the lining in her stomach. She thought she might have heard an odd sound, but at the taut rage in Craig's tone, controlling her nausea took precedence over looking around. ''Where are we going?''

''To the courthouse.''

She swallowed back rising apprehension. ''Why?''

''To get married.''

Relief should have filled her. She wasn't going to jail. He only wanted her to uphold their original bargain. But her reasons for refusing felt even more right now than when she'd first lied about her name.

Stalling to set her racing thoughts in order, she picked up her license and purse, then shoved herself to her feet. ''The only reason you want to marry me is so you'll have a legal claim to the kids.''

''You got that right.''

''You don't need a marriage certificate.'' Thunderclouds darkened his eyes. She tried to explain. ''The kids are yours—''

''Do I look crazy?''

She jerked up her head. ''What are you talking about?''

Out of the corner of her eye, she glimpsed a hint of a dark shadow against the wall. No, she was mistaken. She'd merely seen a contrast between the bright light and the dark paneling. Ignoring the momentary distraction, she allowed his abrupt change of topic to claim her full attention.

"Can you think of even one reason why I should trust you?" he demanded. Craig shook his head in disbelief. Just when he'd begun to think they might have special feelings for one another, he'd discovered she'd lied about her name.

She picked up the pitcher of orange juice. He figured she'd ignore him and fix herself breakfast. Instead, in one smooth motion, as if she was out to kill him, she heaved the full pitcher at his head.

"Duck!" she yelled, her voice hoarse.

Instinctively, he dropped to the floor. Not fast enough. His head exploded in pain. His pulse hammered his eardrums, the roar of a distant dark wave sweeping forward, unstoppable, consuming. Blackness closed in.

HE AWAKENED WITH Summer slapping his face. "Get up. Wake up. He's here. He found us."

Craig's ears rang. His head throbbed as if a jackhammer was pounding his skull. What had happened? The last thing he recalled was Summer tossing the juice pitcher, using his head for target practice. He ought to wring her pretty neck. Lucky for her he hadn't the strength of a ten-year-old.

From his position on the floor, he twisted, ignored the fiery pain and perused the evidence. The pitcher she'd thrown lay shattered near his head. Spilled juice ran in rivulets across the floor, some matting his hair. Or was the sticky sensation blood?

He raised his hand, gingerly touched the lump and pulled back, relieved to see only juice, not blood, on his fingers. Unwilling to reveal any weakness, he kept to himself the eight blurry fingers and two thumbs he counted on one hand.

She shook him. "We have to leave. He could be back any moment."

Fresh pain shocked him out of his stupor. He took in her pinched lips, her chalky face, the gun in her hand. His heart turned cold. First she'd conked him out with a juice pitcher; now she intended to shoot him. Why?

For some reason, he couldn't drum up any fear of her. Instead, disappointment and weariness resonated through him. "Get away from me."

She looked into his eyes and frowned. "Let me help you up. Your eyes aren't focused."

"No kidding. I can't even handle one of you. How do you expect me to handle a duplicate?"

She didn't laugh at his feeble attempt at humor. "You aren't going to pass out on me again, are you?"

He groaned. "What does it matter? Will you shoot me if I refuse to get up?"

She tucked the gun into the waistband of her jeans. "He must have hit you harder than I thought. You aren't making sense."

Neither was she. Hell, what did she expect him to think? He'd regained consciousness to find her holding a gun on him. Mustering the last of his cool, he held back a growl. "Are you saying you didn't hit me with the pitcher?"

"Of course not." Her tone exuded indignation. "*He* came back. How else would I have gotten the gun?"

"Maybe a genie granted you three wishes. Perhaps

the tooth fairy has a wicked sense of humor.'' Craig rolled to his side and held his hand out to her. ''Pull.''

She hauled him up to a sitting position. Once she seemed satisfied he wasn't about to keel over, she headed to the fridge and returned with ice in a plastic bag and wrapped in a towel.

She parted his hair gently. ''You aren't bleeding, but you have a grade-A-egg-size bump.'' She placed the icy towel on his head. ''I'm sorry. I should have reacted faster.''

The pressure hurt, but the ice would reduce the swelling and hopefully the pain. His double vision had already disappeared. ''Tell me what happened.''

''While we were arguing, the stalker must have slipped into the house. The back door is wide open. When he raised the gun over your head, I was afraid if I said something, he'd shoot. So I grabbed the pitcher and threw it. As you ducked, he clubbed you.''

A good thing. His drop to the floor had softened the descending blow. Otherwise, he might still be out cold, maybe dead. ''I remember your throwing the pitcher at my head. I thought I was the target.''

''I missed him, but he slipped in the juice when he ducked. The gun flew from his hand and skidded toward me. I grabbed it and tried to shoot him. The safety was on, and by the time I clicked it off, he'd fled.''

Oddly her far-fetched story had the ring of honesty. Besides, he could see a large orange-juice footprint on the tile floor. She might be telling the truth. Still, after all her lies, he couldn't contain his suspicion. ''What did the intruder look like?''

She sighed but held his gaze. "He wore a ski mask."

"If we luck out, the police can take prints off the weapon."

She folded her arms across her chest. "Going to the police is not an option I want to consider."

For a moment, he debated whether she and a cohort could be conning him. The possibility seemed unlikely. What would be the point?

He thought back carefully to the time when she'd been threatened at the beach. Those shots had come close, but an average marksman shouldn't have missed. The bullets *had* come closer to him than her.

For all he knew, she'd cut up her own underwear and could have bruised her own neck during the party. But she couldn't have feigned her fear, the clammy hands, the fast-beating pulse, the terror in her eyes.

Besides, he couldn't think of any way she could profit from lies about the stalker. Her motive couldn't be money. If it was, she wouldn't have given a fake name on the proxy marriage certificate. She'd have married him legally, then tried to get rid of him to collect. No, whatever she was, she wasn't a fortune hunter.

Which meant she'd probably told the truth. Ever since she'd ridden the motorcycle into his yard, his life had taken twists and turns he hadn't anticipated. Craig liked to plan his life. He didn't appreciate surprises like the stalker's finding them again. He could return at any moment. They had to leave. Fast.

Going to the courthouse for a quickie marriage was also out of the question. The stalker had heard their conversation and might be waiting for them in town.

Summer hunted through a kitchen drawer, picked up a carving knife and advanced on him, halting his thoughts. As if guessing his doubts about her, she handed the knife to him, hilt first. "Keep this. I'll pack, write a note for the kid who takes care of the house and leave him some cash to clean this mess."

Craig tried and failed to rise to his feet. "We need to go now, before the stalker returns with another gun."

"Another five minutes probably won't matter. I doubt he could get his hands on another weapon that quickly. And for all the stalker knows, I've called the cops. Try not to move around too much." She hurried up the steps, her words floating back over her shoulder. "If you pass out on me again, I won't be able to help you into the car."

The thought of rising to his feet made him nauseous. In his present condition, he was much more of a liability than a help to her. "Leave me. Go hide. Keep the babies safe."

She paused on the stairs. "I know you don't think much of me—" her voice cracked, then hardened "—but I'm not leaving you. Now save your breath. I'll be back in a few minutes."

She was as good as her word. At least he thought so. He'd slumped against the side of the counter, may have passed out again. It seemed only moments before she slipped a couple of aspirin into his mouth, gave him water to wash down the pills, then scooted under his arm and urged him to his feet.

She settled her slender arm across his back. "Come on. You can rest in the car."

As they staggered through the door, she removed

the gun from the waistband of her jeans and flipped off the safety. Through his pain-induced stupor, he noted her experience with the handgun and wondered at it.

She lowered him into the passenger seat of the car and headed back to the house to return with their bags and his laptop. After walking around to the driver's side, she placed the gun between them, started the car and backed out of the driveway.

He tried to distract himself from the sickening roiling in his stomach. "When did you learn to use a gun?"

"Gran and I took lessons. She said women living alone are vulnerable. No matter how much we practiced, I always felt uncomfortable owning a weapon. I'm out of practice, though," she admitted. "Kendrick hated guns and didn't want me using one. Naturally, Gran loves them." She pulled into the road, looking left, right and frequently in the rearview mirror. "If you're up to it, I'd like to visit Harry. He may have something important to tell us."

"First, let's stop at the police department." She opened her mouth, but before she could protest, he voiced his compromise. "We'll tell them an intruder hit me from behind and dropped the gun. That information should be enough for them to check for prints and maybe where the gun was last sold."

Summer squirmed in her seat. "Suppose the police don't find any prints on the gun except mine?"

THE POLICE HADN'T really bought their story. At least, that was Summer's impression after she and Craig had handed over the weapon, especially when the officer wanted to know why they'd driven to the station instead of phoning for help. After trying to convince the skeptical policewoman that they were afraid the intruder might return, Summer was anxious to leave the police and their questions behind.

Coming here had been useless. She'd been surprised to learn millions of people had never been fingerprinted. Government workers, military personnel, convicted felons and anyone who had been arrested did have prints on file, but the officer's statistics minimized the likelihood of identifying the intruder from any prints. They should count themselves lucky they hadn't been seriously hurt or robbed, she'd said.

The Automated Fingerprint Identification System would take less than twenty-four hours to process any prints from the gun. With a minor miracle, they'd have a match. Meanwhile, their hopes of a quick solution squelched, they drove to Harry's office to find out why he wanted to see Summer. She'd offered to drop Craig at a hotel so he could lie down, but despite his obvious pain, he refused to leave her side.

Her former boss had insisted he couldn't spare time for a lunch meeting, and his secretary sent them into his office the moment they arrived. Summer would have recognized Harry's disorganized mess anywhere. Folders from file cabinets overflowed, spreading across every surface from the desk to the windowsills and onto the floor in a manila wave. Summer and Craig wound their way through piles of documents to reach the two chairs facing Harry's desk.

"Come in. Glad you could make it. How's your neck?" He peered at Summer's bruises while moving papers off the chairs so they could sit. "Coffee?"

"No thanks," she answered, eager for him to get to the point.

In his usual brisk manner, Harry's greeting had jumped from subject to subject, but today he sounded nervous as well as overworked. His eyes darted from her to Craig and back as if afraid of their reaction.

Harry's delay in reaching the point of their meeting unnerved her. She had no time for social amenities. "Why did you ask us to come here? Is there a problem with a case I worked on?"

"Nothing like that. Your work was impeccable, always neat and organized." He threw his hands up in the air. "I really have to straighten out these files. But then how would I find anything?"

Beside her, Craig stretched out his feet, his brow raised at Harry's remark. Craig's restrained silence was admirable. Or perhaps pain, not self-control, prevented him from saying much. Either way, he seemed content to let her carry the conversation.

Harry peered at her through his glasses. "I had a break-in last week. As far as I can tell, the only item stolen was the file concerning your parents' estate."

How odd. Her parents hadn't owned anything of value. Perhaps the thief had made a mistake. Or maybe Harry had simply misplaced the file. In this mess, losing paperwork seemed more likely than a theft.

"Are you sure?" she asked.

"I may appear disorganized, but I brought out that file just last week when your uncle Bob came to see me."

Summer rubbed her brow. "Did his visit have anything to do with me?"

Harry planted his elbows on his desk and knitted his fingers together. "That's just it—I don't know. Bob had been drinking. He kept grumbling about those stock certificates your father was supposedly holding for him."

Craig leaned forward. His eyes gleamed with sudden interest. "Are you saying old stock certificates are just left lying around in your files?"

Harry bristled. "Absolutely not. The estate had few assets that I could find. No stock certificates were mentioned. After your parent's deaths, I meticulously read all the paperwork, everything but your mother's diary."

A diary? The existence of such a memento stunned her. Her only memories of her mother were from Gran's stories. To hold her mother's diary, to read her words, would have given her immense pleasure. "She left me a diary?"

"According to the will you are supposed to receive all personal items when you turn thirty."

"Why so long?"

Harry shrugged. "That's a moot point now."

"The diary was stolen?" Sorrow filled Summer at the loss.

"Did the diary refer to the stock certificates?" Craig asked.

Harry pinched the bridge of his nose. "After Bob mentioned the stock certificates, I read the diary twice. I assure you, the certificates were never even alluded to."

Summer recalled how Uncle Bob always needed money. "You think Bob didn't believe you and broke into your office to steal the file?"

"The thought occurred to me." Harry rose from his chair, walked around his desk and patted her back. "I thought you should know. I intended to tell you at the party but didn't have the chance. After you were attacked, I wondered if the same person might be behind these seemingly unconnected incidents."

Summer stood and hugged Harry. "Now you have me wondering, too. Thanks for letting me know."

Craig shook Harry's hand. "Just one more question. Have you ever been fingerprinted?"

"No, why?"

"It's not important," Craig told him.

As she and Craig walked out of the office building into L.A.'s smog, Summer felt as though the air was being sucked from her lungs. She had to talk to Gran, but Craig looked so weary, she hated to drag him to the nursing home. "Do you think it's safe to visit Gran?"

"Why?"

"I want to ask her a few questions about Uncle Bob and the stock he mentioned."

"A call from a pay phone would be safer. I'd recommend keeping the conversation short—no more than three minutes, so the call can't be traced."

His responses were brief, cold, as if he cared nothing for her, as if they'd never made love. His attitude clearly said he'd help her protect his babies, but anything more between them was off-limits.

Right now, her concern revolved around the past. She pulled into the first service station she saw with a pay phone. Grabbing a handful of change from her purse, she punched Gran's number.

"Hi, Gran."

"Are you all right?" Gran's voice revealed no signs of sleepiness. "I was so worried after the party. I know it's hard for you to call."

"Sorry." To her long list of faults, Summer guiltily added another for making her grandmother worry. "I can't talk more than a few minutes. I went to see Harry Pibbs. He told me my parents' file was stolen from his office."

"After all this time?"

"Uncle Bob visited Harry just last week and asked about those missing stock certificates again."

"You know better than to listen to Bob's ramblings. For years after your father died, Bob claimed your father owed him money. He said your dad kept the certificates in a safe place, probably to prevent him from drinking up the profits."

"So you don't know if my father bought stock or not?"

"Your father buy stock?" Gran snorted. "My son was a straight arrow. He believed investing in other people's businesses akin to gambling."

Perhaps the break-in had nothing to do with her uncle. "So Uncle Bob's story is impossible?"

Gran paused for a moment. "Come to think of it, your mother occasionally dabbled in the market. I seem to recall reading something about stocks in her diary. You're supposed to receive it when you—"

"Wait a second." Summer's heartbeat accelerated with excitement. "Harry just told me there wasn't a word in Mom's diary about stocks."

"He did?" Doubt filled Gran's voice. "Maybe I'm wrong."

"Think, Gran."

"I could have sworn I read about your mother's investments somewhere. Maybe I'm mistaken. She died a long time ago."

From the car, Craig motioned Summer to cut the call short. Quickly she asked Gran to give her directions to Uncle Bob's house im Santa Barbara.

"Gran, thanks. I don't know when I can call again."

"I understand."

"Gran, was Uncle Bob ever fingerprinted?"

"I don't know. Be careful. I love you, honey."

"Love you, too, Gran." She hung up the phone and hurried back to Craig. After repeating the conversation, she waited for his take on the situation.

His face remained unreadable. "You said Harry needed money years ago when he started his business, right?"

"You think Harry took the stock?"

"He had opportunity and motive."

She breathed deeply, then slowly exhaled. "Even if he did, that doesn't make him the stalker."

"Unless he was trying to distract you from the missing stock by giving you bigger problems to think about."

"But Harry has always been so good to me."

"Maybe he feels guilty. The timing seems right, too. Didn't the stalking begin shortly after you called and asked Harry if there was any truth to the missing stock?"

While she disagreed with Craig's analysis, at least he was talking to her. An afternoon and evening without tension might restore any goodwill he had left toward her. With that goal in mind, she pulled out of the gas station. There was no sign of anyone following.

Still, her neck prickled as if someone was watching.

A good night's sleep in wine country would leave them well rested. With no bolt-hole ready for them to hide in, they couldn't turn back. If she had to, she'd drive like a crazy woman, lose the tail.

The past weeks on the run had toughened her. Fear wouldn't stop her. Neither would Craig. She was tired of running, tired of being a coward.

Craig's cold and silent treatment wouldn't defeat her. She wanted answers. And she was willing to risk another encounter with her stalker to get them. Anything to get her life back.

Tonight, she'd stay with Craig, make sure he recovered. She owed him that much. Tomorrow, she'd confront Uncle Bob. If necessary, she'd face him alone.

Chapter Ten

California vineyards were renowned for producing some of the finest wines in the world. While the northern vintners grew most of the wine grapes, others had discovered pockets of land where soil and climate matched the growing conditions up north. Santa Barbara, where Bob Carlson lived, was one of those pockets.

The day before, Summer and Craig had driven north on the Hollywood Freeway. They had spent the night in Ojai, a sleepy artists' and writers' colony hidden away on the edge of the Los Padres National Forest.

Summer had thought Craig should have spent the afternoon recuperating in bed from his head injury, but he'd worked through most of the day and into the evening, faxing directions to his staff and catching up on E-mail through his computer modem.

This morning, Craig, mostly recovered, was back behind the wheel, driving North on Highway 101. His attitude toward her hadn't changed, and his polite indifference irritated her. Not that she had a choice, but she'd rather he'd yell at her than ignore her. Since she hadn't worked up the courage to deliberately start an argument, the car remained silent, the air between them fraught with tension.

They took the main street out of town past the graceful tower that offset a row of unpretentious shops under a covered veranda. She didn't break the silence between them until they arrived on the outskirts of Santa Barbara.

When Uncle Bob *had* a job, he worked unusual hours, and she hoped to catch him at home. Summer stretched her legs, anxious to get the visit over with. "Bob lives between the wharf and downtown, a little north of the city."

Craig turned at the corner of State and Victoria. "We should have called first."

"I don't want to give him any warning. If he did steal the file and my mother's diary from Harry's office, he might leave it in sight. If we warn him, he'll have time to hide the evidence."

"You think he's the stalker?"

"What would be the point? What motive could he possibly have?"

The contrast between the quiet tension in the car and the humming activity around an outdoor fountain in the attractive town where tourists and locals sipped coffee increased Summer's awareness of how out of kilter her life had tipped. In another minute or so, they'd reach the area where State Street terminated at Stearns Wharf, but they wouldn't be visiting any of the tourist attractions. Instead, she was considering whether or not her uncle could be her stalker.

Craig avoided a skater and smoothly changed lanes. "Let's suppose the stock certificates he asked Harry about actually exist. Suppose they've appreciated over the years and become valuable. If he thinks you have them, maybe he'd come after you.''

"If I had them, I would have sold them to pay for law school. He's aware of my tight financial situation. Besides, if the stock certificates aren't a figment of his imagination, why would Uncle Bob warn me at a party to get rid of you and the babies?''

"Perhaps he thinks you'll sell the stock and spend the money on your new family. Unless your grandmother told him, he doesn't know the conditions of our agreement.''

"Gran wouldn't tell.'' Spotting the adobe bell towers her grandmother had told her to watch for when she'd given directions, Summer checked the map on her lap. "Make your first right, then go about a mile. His house should be on the right.''

"Maybe Bob thinks you spent his share of the stock and is after you for revenge.''

She sighed. "I suppose it's possible. But why would he keep bringing up the subject if he believes we already spent the money?''

"Who can tell what goes on in the mind of an alcoholic? Has your uncle ever been arrested? Fingerprinted?'' Craig asked.

"I asked Gran and she didn't know. But when I was a kid, Gran tried to keep him away from me. She didn't approve of his drinking.''

"What's he do for a living?''

"He's a salesman. Actually, he's quite good at it while he's on the wagon. He's sold everything from radio advertising to used cars. Lately, he's into multi-level marketing. He never lasts long once his bosses find out about his drinking problem. That's when he comes around asking for handouts.''

Craig's fingers clenched around the wheel. "Do you have any enemies you haven't told me about?''

"Enemies?'' His question revealed his distrust and left the taste of ashes in her mouth. She supposed since she'd lied about her name, he thought she'd lied about her entire life. Whatever fires had been kindled between them, she had extinguished. "I've led a quiet life. Until the stalker pursued me, nothing unusual happened in my entire life.''

"Losing both parents in a car accident is unusual. Perhaps the events now are connected to the past.''

She closed the map and replaced it in the glove compartment. "After all this time? I don't think so.''

Bob Carlson's house, painted a light tan, stood at the end of a short grass driveway, its front so veiled by showering gold-green foliage of weeping willows that Summer glimpsed only a hint of the rambling, nondescript stucco house. Except for a flower box with marigolds, it closely resembled the other homes on the block.

Craig pulled into the driveway. She unbuckled her seat belt. "I'd pictured his house differently.''

"How so?''

"My memories of Uncle Bob are almost all unpleasant. I thought he would live in a bare, dank apartment.''

They strode to the door, maintaining a clear-cut space between them. Except when he'd had to rely on her due to his injury, Craig hadn't touched her since he'd discovered her real last name.

She wouldn't lie to herself. Their relationship

wasn't better this way. Although they'd been together practically every moment, his withdrawal hurt. Once again, the sting of self-doubt tortured her. Had she been selfish, taking more from him than she'd given back?

Even now in his remoteness, he treated her politely, which almost made the pain worse. She missed imparting her thoughts, missed the warmth in his eyes when he gazed at her, missed his caresses. Craig had unstintingly set time aside to assist her. He had held her and told her he enjoyed their lovemaking. He had protected her, never letting her out of shouting-for-help distance. They had shared so much. Whatever she'd meant to him—and she was never really sure what he saw in her besides the children—she'd ruined by her lies.

Yet Craig was still there for her, keeping her focused on finding the stalker, paying attention to her ideas and helping her face the danger. But the emotional distance he kept between them made her uncomfortable. Still, she welcomed his company. Facing Uncle Bob wouldn't be easy. Having Craig with her gave her courage.

She rang the bell. In her nervousness, she reached for Craig's hand without thinking. Before they touched, she recalled their argument and his changed feelings toward her. Hoping he hadn't noticed her instinctive response to needing him, she dispiritedly dropped her arm to her side.

She rang the bell again. Craig banged with the knocker.

They waited. She tried not to hold her breath. "Maybe he's not home."

Craig pounded with his fist.

"I'm coming," Bob shouted grumpily from the other side of the door.

The longer he took, the tighter her nerves rolled up. What was taking him so long?

Finally, a dead bolt clicked. The door opened soundlessly.

Bob ran a hand over his unshaven jaw, prickly with a mixture of white and gray bristles. Wearing a cream polo shirt and navy slacks, shoes but no socks, he stepped back and squinted against the bright light.

Craig's voice was neutral and pleasant. "Good morning."

"Could we talk?" Summer asked hesitantly.

Bob swung the door wide. "Come in and I'll make some coffee."

His gracious welcome settled her frazzled nerves but heightened her suspicions. She glanced over at Craig as she entered the neatly kept house. If he was surprised, he was doing a good job of hiding it.

Bob led them into a faded but spotless yellow kitchen that looked onto a patio. A bird feeder hung from the limb of an orange tree. A chess set sat on a table between two iron chairs with soft yellow cushions.

Summer and Craig seated themselves in swivel chairs at the breakfast bar while Bob heated water, measured coffee and turned on the percolator. Without looking at them, he took out a sugar bowl from a cabinet, poured milk into a creamer and set black cups and saucers on the white counter.

He peered into the freezer. "I've got some coffee cake in here somewhere."

"That's okay," Summer said, not the least bit hungry.

"It's really no trouble," Bob insisted, his hands shifting items around in the freezer. "Aha!"

He pulled out a foil-covered package, removed the wrapping and placed the cake on a glass plate in the microwave. She hadn't expected to be welcomed. Certainly not with coffee cake. Her uncle's abilities as a host had thrown her, but then she supposed survival as a bachelor necessitated some domestic talent.

The scent of the defrosting cake mixed with the perking coffee. In the cozy kitchen, Summer suddenly realized as much as she wanted to identify her stalker, she didn't want him to be Uncle Bob. Seeing him puttering around his home, pouring them coffee, she couldn't imagine him shooting at her on the beach, strangling her at the party or frightening her with threatening notes.

Bob peered over his coffee cup, his arthritic hands shaky, but his eyes sharp. "So to what do I owe the honor of this visit?"

After seeing this new side of her uncle, she didn't want to break the peaceful atmosphere with wild accusations. Delaying, she sipped and set the cup back in the saucer before answering, determined to watch his eyes as he responded. "We visited Harry Pibbs yesterday. He said you'd been asking after my parents' file."

"That's correct. Did he tell you why?" Bob met her gaze with a directness that puzzled her. This meeting wasn't going the way she'd thought. She hadn't expected him to admit so easily to requesting the file.

Craig swallowed a bite of cake, not the least bit

reticent about getting down to business. "He mentioned you were looking for stock certificates."

"That's right." Although he hadn't drained his
cup, Bob poured more coffee. "No one believes me,
not even my sister, but before Summer's parents died,
we invested in some stock. I was drinking a lot back
then, and Summer's mother suggested she hold on to
the certificates for me."

"How much did you invest?" Craig asked.

A wry grin curled Bob's lips. "Not much. We each
put in a few hundred dollars."

"The stock went up," Summer guessed.

"I don't know."

Summer's brow furrowed as she attempted to fit
the pieces of the puzzle together. An investment of a
few hundred dollars couldn't account for Bob's interest in the stock twenty years later. Nor did it explain
why a thief would steal the file out of Harry's office.

Perhaps she'd misunderstood. "We're not talking
about a huge amount of money, are we?" Summer
asked.

Bob chuckled. "That's the mystery. I have no idea
which stock your mother bought."

Summer sighed.

Craig didn't look pleased. His chin cocked at a
skeptical angle. "Do you have proof any stock was
bought?"

For the first time, Bob wouldn't meet their eyes but
stared into the depths of his coffee. "I've searched
for the missing papers for twenty years. I've never
found them."

She sensed Uncle Bob was holding back. "There's
something I don't understand. This house, the

stock...I always thought you were broke. Why do you come around asking Gran for ten dollars here, twenty there?"

Bob's face flushed crimson and he ducked his head in embarrassment. "I don't drink all the time. But when I do, I binge. I'll do anything, spend anything, for the next drink. I have friends who mete out my own money to me. It's the only way I've managed to control my habit."

The plan made sense. His answer explained why he wore nice clothes, had a good haircut, but didn't have money in his pocket. Now she realized that the only time she'd seen him had been during a drinking binge.

Craig put the conversation back on track. "Harry's office was broken into last week. Summer's parents' file was stolen."

Bob shook his head, his ruddy complexion turning pasty gray. "Because I asked about the diary, you think I stole the file?"

Tension filled a long moment of silence.

"It *is* a big coincidence," Summer finally said gently, wishing she could squeeze Craig's hand under the counter.

"I wasn't going to show you...but since you already think I'm guilty, what harm can it do?" Bob shoved away his coffee and stood. "Come with me."

Summer's heart beat like a trip-hammer. She had no idea what he was about to show them, but perhaps another piece of the puzzle would solve the mystery. Were the missing stock and the stalker somehow connected?

Bob led them through a narrow hall into a dark

study. Shelves filled with books lined one wall. Just like the rest of the house, the room was neat. Not one paper was on the desk, no mail, no magazines, not even a crooked family picture. Bob pulled a chain dangling from an emerald-shaded desk lamp and cast murky light into the dim shadows.

He opened the top right drawer and, without hesitation, pulled out a manila envelope. "I shouldn't have taken this. I hope you'll understand why I did."

Summer's mouth went dry. In her eagerness to see the contents, her fingers trembled as she took the envelope and poured the contents onto Bob's desk. Two faded sheets of odd-size paper fluttered out. Along one yellowed edge, the paper was ragged as if torn out of a notebook. A neat script in blue ink filled the lines.

Craig bent over at the same time she did. Their heads almost touched.

"What is this?" Craig asked.

"Shortly after Summer's parents died, I broke into the house while she and my sister were out shopping."

Summer gasped. Gran had known someone had been in the house. Afterward, her grandmother had learned how to shoot. Later, she'd insisted Summer learn, too.

"You were looking for the stock certificates?" Craig asked, his voice neutral.

Bob replied in a rush, his tone a plea for understanding and forgiveness. "I only wanted the half I was due. But when I couldn't find any stock certificates, I read your mother's diary looking for clues. I ripped out these two pages. I took nothing else, I swear it.''

Summer frowned. "But if you'd already read the diary, why did you ask Harry if you could see it again?"

"I thought I might have overlooked a clue in the first read. But I didn't have to steal the diary. I *was* already fairly sure I wouldn't find anything. I just needed to be certain."

While she and Bob spoke, Craig read the two pages of the diary. "These words prove nothing."

Bob slapped his palm on the desk. "It proves her mother and I invested in stock."

Summer's legs collapsed under her, and she sank into a chair. She had few direct memories of her parents, and Gran's stories had depicted her mother as a woman who was more interested in art and music than investments. Could this business side of her mother's personality explain her own interest in pursuing a career like law?

She mentally reviewed what Bob had told them. If he'd searched Gran's house, had he done the same to her place? "Did you ransack my apartment looking for the stock?"

"No."

"Have you been following me, watching to see if I found the certificates and cashed them in?"

"Of course not," he answered indignantly. "I have better things to do than follow you around. Besides, I think I know who has the certificates."

Her heart somersaulted into her throat. "Who?"

"Harry Pibbs."

The stunning aftershock of his words left her numb

with his revelation and sinking deeper into the chair. The kindly attorney who'd looked after her parents' estate, who'd hired her, who occasionally took Gran out to dinner, had stolen their stock certificates? "I don't believe it."

"You don't *want* to believe he did it," Bob said.

"Harry had the opportunity," Craig added. "If the stock was among your parents' papers, he could have stolen them, believing no one would notice."

"Exactly." Bob's voice rose an octave. "I knew the certificates existed, but who would believe a drunk? Harry could have cashed the stock in and no one would have been the wiser."

Summer's head spun. "I don't know. Nothing makes sense. If Harry stole the certificates, do you think he's also stalking me? What would be his motive?"

Bob frowned. "Stalking you?"

Craig spent the next few minutes explaining the situation to Bob. When Craig had finished, her uncle appeared just as baffled as Summer.

"Maybe the missing stock has nothing to do with the stalker," Craig suggested, his tone even.

At the square set of his broad shoulders and the diamond glint in his dark eyes, a sharp shiver ran up her spine. "Do you believe that?"

"I don't know what I think."

He'd answered her question about the stalker, but from his wary look, she suspected he'd spoken about her entire situation. His comment was the first crack in his armor. That he hadn't made up his mind gave her room for a tiny spark of hope to flicker deep inside her. Perhaps Craig hadn't totally closed her out of his life.

"The two of you are welcome to spend a few days here," Bob offered, his voice almost a lonely plea. "I have extra bedrooms. Not many people stop by."

Bob seemed pathetically eager for them to remain, but she'd never sleep under his roof, not until they identified the stalker. She still wasn't convinced her uncle was innocent. He'd ripped pages out of her mother's diary. He'd been in Harry's office a week before the file mysteriously vanished. He'd also been at the party. He knew where Gran lived and could have followed Summer after every visit. No, she didn't trust Uncle Bob. Staying could be dangerous.

Without her saying a word, Craig seemed to read her thoughts. He turned to her uncle. "On the way over, we could have been followed. We won't put you in danger."

"No one's coming after me. Stay. Let me put you up for the night."

Bob seemed so sincere, Summer almost gave in. But she couldn't jeopardize the babies. "Another time maybe. Please understand. We'll be safer if we keep moving."

SUMMER AND CRAIG might be physically safer if they kept driving, but emotionally, Summer was a wreck. "Can we talk?" she asked.

"There's nothing to say."

"I'd like to explain why—"

"I don't want to hear it." His voice was even, as if he no longer cared about her. Her stomach heaved and she fought to keep down the coffee she'd just drunk.

Whether the reason for the emotional upset was due to her pregnancy and raging hormones, or because she was tired of running, no longer mattered. With all her problems, she couldn't stand the difficulties between her and Craig. The constant worrying had worn her down, and she didn't know what to say or do to make things right between them.

"Stop the car, please. I need to call Gran."

Without a word, Craig pulled into a shopping center. He parked and started to get out of the car.

She couldn't think of a polite way to get rid of him for the next few minutes. Almost choking on the words, knowing her request would make Craig distrust her even more, she gathered her courage. "I'd like some privacy."

"Don't stay on the phone long." Craig stabbed her with a piercing look, shoved his hands into his pockets and walked away, shaking his head.

He probably didn't realize how cold he sounded. Craig just wanted her to be careful. Calls could be traced.

Summer punched in numbers barely visible through eyes brimming with moisture. She brushed away a tear. It seemed forever until Gran answered.

"Gran!"

"You sound upset. Are you okay? Where are you?"

"We just saw Uncle Bob and we're heading back to L.A."

"Why are you crying?" Gran asked.

Summer gripped the phone, wishing she could hug

her grandmother instead. The stalker, the pregnancy, her fight with Craig, all caught up with her. She was a mass of miserable confusion without a clue how to straighten out the mess she'd created. "Craig found out I lied to him about my name. He's furious. He thinks I plan to take the babies away."

"Is he treating you okay?"

The words poured out in a rush. "He's been so cold. He won't talk to me about anything personal. I don't know how to break through."

"Where are you staying tonight?"

"I don't know. We'll probably find somewhere along the coast. Why?"

"Because the easiest way to break down a man's resistance is with actions, not words."

"What are you saying?"

"Girl, you spent too much time studying for your classes and worrying over me to know what to do with a real man. Go to him."

"He won't listen."

Gran chuckled. "Take him to bed."

Summer almost dropped the phone. "I couldn't."

"Sure you can."

She gulped. Gran didn't understand that Craig no longer wanted her. Desperation made her speak the truth. "He doesn't want me. Not like that."

"I've seen the way he looks at you. He wants you. Don't give him a chance to remember he's mad."

"Huh?"

Gran chuckled again, planning strategy like a general. "Wait until he's asleep. Sneak under the covers. Let nature take its course."

And like a good soldier, Summer would try to obey orders, but where would she find the courage to follow through? "I don't know, Gran."

From across the parking lot, Craig motioned Summer to hurry.

"For once in your life, take a chance. He's a good man. If you let him get away, you'll regret missing this opportunity for the rest of your life."

When Summer didn't hang up, Craig walked over.

Quickly, she whispered into the mouthpiece, "I'll think about what you said."

"Oh, one other thing."

"Yes?" she said hesitantly, imagining Gran's twinkling eyes and her cheeky grin.

"When you climb into his bed, make sure you don't have any clothes on."

Chapter Eleven

With Gran's words in mind, Summer chose Simpson House for her seduction, hoping one of the loveliest places in Santa Barbara would lend her courage and put Craig in a romantic mood. The grand Eastlake-style Victorian stood secluded behind wrought-iron gates and high hedges on nearly an acre of majestic oak, pittosporum and magnolia trees.

Her elegant room had a brass bed with a down comforter under a lace coverlet. Instead of allowing the antique furniture and Oriental rug of the luxurious room to soothe her, her attention was drawn like a magnet to the connecting door to Craig's room. Could she step over the threshold tonight, put her fears behind her and open her heart to Craig? With him, everything seemed possible and within reach.

She'd always closed herself off to protect herself from the eventual pain of abandonment. The foundations of the self-protective mechanisms guarding her heart had been laid the first time she'd been old enough to ask Gran why her mom and dad had to die. That child had had a big hollow place inside her that couldn't be filled. She'd lie still and quiet wrapped in her mother's sweater, wondering what she had said or done to make them leave her. If she tried really hard, she could smell her mother's scent, and then with the faintest whiff of wildflowers around her, she'd cry herself to sleep.

More walls went up when her grandfather died. Most recently, Kendrick's self-centered behavior had locked the door. Now she had to break free and risk a full commitment to love.

Despite the unbreachable walls, she was already in love with Craig. She'd just been afraid to face her feelings. Or the fear that she might want him in a way he didn't want her.

She had to find out. She couldn't live with herself if she didn't.

"I love him." In the empty room, she said the words aloud, liking their feel and taste on her tongue.

At the bay window, she stared into the rose garden below, but she couldn't shake the mental image of that closed door. To cross the threshold, she had to open the door wide. She had to expose her emotions. Go for broke.

Like a prisoner kept in a cell her entire life, she feared leaving what she knew. At the same time, a whole world awaited her if she dared to take a chance.

Nothing in her past had prepared her for this moment because she'd never felt so excited or so vulnerable before. Even if Craig never loved her in return, he'd taught her to dream. She wouldn't look back.

The jitters zinging through her were symptoms of self-doubt mixed with excited anticipation. Although she had no idea where she'd find the nerve to pull off a seduction, the new feelings propelled her to her duffel bag.

She recalled Gran's instructions and grinned. At least she didn't have to worry over what to wear. But that didn't mean she couldn't smell wonderful. After a shower, she dried her hair and brushed it until her dark locks shone. No wig tonight. She would go to him without disguise.

Craig buzzed her room to ask if she was ready for dinner. Knowing she couldn't eat, she declined. If he was disappointed, he hid his feelings well.

"I was going to tell you over dinner..." His voice was as smooth as fine brandy and just as enticing.

She ignored the heat curling in her stomach at the sound of his voice. Thankful he couldn't see her nervous gesture, she drummed her nails on the vanity. "Tell me what?"

"You sure you won't eat something?" he coaxed.

"I'm bushed. I thought I'd take a nap. Maybe have a bowl of soup later in front of the TV."

"You aren't sick?"

"I'm fine. The babies are fine. What was it you wanted to tell me?"

"The police didn't find any prints on the gun except yours."

After he hung up, she was sorry she hadn't gone to dinner to distract herself from the disappointment of his news. The lovely room seemed empty. Contemplating what would happen later had her muscles in a coil. She threw herself on the bed, never expecting to fall asleep. But she must have been more tired than she'd realized.

She awakened at midnight with the full moon shimmering through the window, the scent of roses in the air, her pulse fluttering. Time to go after what she wanted. Eager to put her plan into action before she lost her courage, she tossed back the covers and stood.

Had Craig returned to his room and fallen asleep? She'd curl up and die if she walked into his room as bare as a nudist while he was awake.

She'd never in her life done anything as bold as entering a man's room naked. The moonlight coming through the window bathed her in its soft white glow. A soft breeze prickled her skin. She'd never felt so vulnerable, either. Inhaling a deep breath, she let out the air slowly.

There's a first time for everything.

Pride held her back and shoulders erect as she walked to the door separating their rooms. She reached for the knob. Hesitated. She couldn't move. Her feet grew roots. If panic hadn't overwhelmed her, she would have dived back under the covers.

You can do this. Stop acting like a terrified virgin.

But suppose he refused her?

Suppose he didn't?

She had no idea how long she stood on icy feet, her heart pounding, goose bumps lining up on her bare skin. If she stood still much longer before going to him, he'd think an icicle had climbed into his bed.

She'd enticed him once before by playing the beguiling temptress, and she could do it again now that the stakes were so much higher. Only this time, she wouldn't be pretending she wanted him. This time, her love was real. She was feeling so much and the emotion was all so new, she couldn't bear the thought of failing.

She yanked open the door, wincing at the tiny squeak. Except for the antiques, his room was identical to hers. He'd even drawn back the drapes and moonlight was flooding the room.

Focusing on the dark shape on the bed, she approached on tiptoe. He lay sleeping on his back, one arm flung over his face, the other resting on his stomach, the sheet covering him from the waist down.

Slowly, ever so carefully, she scooted onto the mattress.

He smelled so good, clean and male and exotic, like a fresh-mown lawn under a forest of pine with a hint of incendiary balsam.

She rubbed her hands on her hips to warm them before she dared touch him. Where to start?

In the moonlight, his face was a contrast of light and shadow. His dark hair spiked against the whiteness of the pillow, and she delicately ran her fingers through it. God, he was hot. Heat radiated off his flesh, and for a moment she feared he was sick, then her chattering teeth told her she was cold.

She snuggled her head against his chest, and his heated skin was a delicious contrast to her cool flesh, stirring singing desire. Lying beside him felt so right. Even asleep, Craig seemed to agree. The arm that had been resting on his face slipped down to curl over her shoulders, drawing her near. His breathing remained even, and she briefly wondered who was with him in his dreams.

Not that it mattered. She was here. In his bed. Letting nature take its course.

Nature couldn't show him how she felt. She'd have to do that herself. She skimmed her fingers along his jaw, down his chest and stomach. Lower.

Craig might still be sleeping, but one part of his anatomy was most definitely awake. She trailed her fingers over his arousal, pleased when he leaped at her delicate caresses.

A smile on her lips, she pressed tiny kisses to his shoulder and chest. He moaned softly as if asking for more. She was ready to give him more, ready to give him everything she had without qualifications, without reservations.

She let her lips follow the path her hand had taken. He let out a glorious sigh, and she gave herself up to waking him in a way that would bring him the most pleasure, in a way he couldn't refuse.

Kissing him deeply, hungrily, unhurriedly, she cherished her feminine powers. This was a side of herself she'd been fighting because she was afraid of how she felt, afraid she would lose control, afraid once she began she wouldn't be able to stop no matter how much she tried. But love wasn't something to be controlled. Love had set her free.

She reveled in the tightness of her stomach, the chanting heat in her blood and in the pulse-pounding certainty that she wanted to spend the rest of her life with this man.

His hands tightened in her hair, and she sensed he'd awakened. "How...what...?" He groaned. "You feel good."

When he didn't send her away, she shivered, and an electrifying pleasure surged through her. He confirmed he wanted her by softly kneading her neck, caressing her shoulders.

"Come here," he commanded in a voice throaty with need that drew her upward. She straddled his hips, wiggled and failed to get him inside her. "Not yet."

"But—"

"Don't move," he told her. "Or I won't be responsible for what happens."

Pleased she had him on the brink, she did as he asked. He reached for her breasts and the heat from his palms licked a fire all the way to her heart.

"Tell me why you're here," he crooned huskily, while his magical hands excited and pleasured her breasts.

"I can't concentrate when you touch me like that."

"Good." She sensed his smile from his tone, his satisfaction from his ragged breathing.

She gyrated her hips in a blatant attempt to capture his heat.

He plucked at her nipple, shooting aching need between her thighs. "You didn't answer my question. Why are you here?"

"Because I want you."

His hands returned to stroking her breasts. "Why?"

"I feel good when I'm with you."

He was driving her wild with his teasing hands, his difficult questions. She'd never felt so excited or frustrated in her life. Being so close to having what she wanted created a humming tension. His arousal pulsed beneath her parted thighs. So close, but so far.

He dropped his hands from her breasts and caressed

the insides of her knees. "So this is about my skill as a lover?"

"No."

"You don't like what I'm doing to you?"

"Yes. No. I don't know. I can't think when you touch me like that."

He inched his fingertips along, drawing slow circles on the sensitive skin of her inner thighs. Each feathery caress advanced a little farther, a little closer to where she waited for him, open, vulnerable, trembling. He'd already touched her heart. Now she would give him the rest of her.

She no longer had a choice. As she took in his wonderful scent with every breath, every nerve ending fired with longing.

When she didn't think she could wait another moment, he fondled her where she most wanted to be touched. His intimate caresses had become as necessary as breathing. Nothing had ever felt so wonderful. The tension pressing her lungs tautly constricted. She couldn't catch her breath. Her head reeled.

He planted a searing kiss on her nipple. His hot fingers teased and burned. Every inch of her buzzed with sizzling electricity. With a moan of surprise, she spasmed in mind-blowing pleasure. When his fingers kept up their tempo, combustible pleasure left her gasping. She hadn't known she could feel so hot, so joyous, so filled with passion.

"I'm not done with you."

"Good." She lifted her hips, knowing with Craig there could be still more. "I want you inside me."

He granted her wish a moment later, filling her completely. They joined as close as man and woman could come. His hands moved over her bottom, helping her find a rhythm. She marveled how free she felt to take what he had to give, how he accepted all she was willing to offer.

The tempo increased. Rational thought fled with the fullness of him inside her, under her, stroking her. He let go of her bottom and his fingers found her core. She exploded again. This time, the pleasure left her dizzy.

She collapsed atop his chest and he embraced her, his hands smoothing the hair off her face, caressing her shoulder and stroking her back. Snuggling against him, triumphant and happily exhausted, she knew coming to him had been the right thing to do.

He kissed her. Kissed her as if she was the most important thing in his world. "That was a fantastic way to wake-up."

"I was afraid you would refuse me." She heard him choke back a chuckle and grinned. "Gran knew better."

He tightened his arms around her. "What do you mean?"

A woman had to keep some secrets. She had no intention of admitting that she'd climbed into his bed at Gran's urging. "Gran gave me a little advice."

"And what was that?"

Summer giggled. "I can't remember her exact words."

"Try."

"She encouraged me to go after what I wanted. And what I wanted was you."

He tipped up her head for a kiss. "Well, you certainly had me."

CRAIG PACED restlessly in Gran's small living room. On the couch beside her grandmother, Summer sat curled up with the Siamese cat on her lap, her incredible legs tucked beneath her. In his tennis whites, Fred sat opposite the women. He kept glancing at his watch as if he didn't want to be late for a lesson.

"Gran, are all of my mother's things packed away in storage?"

She had told Craig after she'd decided to move out of Gran's house, Gran had moved here. Summer couldn't bear to sell their old home, so they'd rented the house and put most of their possessions in storage.

"I'm afraid there's not much left after all these years."

Fred picked up his tennis racket and his fingers plucked the strings. "What about all that junk in the attic?"

Summer smiled at Fred. "You remember when we used to play up there when we were kids?"

"Sure do. You'd dress in your mom's clothes and pretend you were a queen."

"The two of them spent hours up there," Gran told Craig.

Someday, Craig wanted a little girl just like Summer, who played dress-up. After the way she'd responded to him last night, he thought she was finally ready to listen to what he had to say.

Right now, as she petted the cat, she looked more content than he'd ever seen her. The tight wariness had lifted from her eyes, replaced by a soft, shimmering sparkle. Her lips smiled more easily, and as he recalled just where those lips had been and how they'd felt, he knew he had to leave before he embarrassed himself.

Summer should be safe with her grandmother. Even if Fred left for a lesson, security had been instructed not to let anyone into the building without checking identification before buzzing open the door. The neighbors had been alerted to strangers who might use sneak tactics to worm their way inside.

"While you all try to figure out where Summer's mother hid the stock certificates," Craig said, "I have a few errands to run."

Fred rose to his feet. "I've got to leave, too. My eleven o'clock's waiting."

Summer nodded to them both. "Go on. We'll be fine."

"I'll be back soon." Craig bent and gave her a goodbye kiss. "It shouldn't take long to drive to my office, sign the new import contracts and return."

Summer handed the cat to Gran and walked the men to the door. "Don't worry. I won't open the door for strangers, and I'll lock the door behind you."

Craig waited for the dead bolt to click before he hurried out of the building. He looked at his watch. Just enough time to do a little shopping and surprise Summer.

From the sunlit parking lot, he counted up two stories and the requisite number of windows over to find Summer and her grandmother standing at the window and waving a cheery farewell. He waved back and opened his car door. And halted.

A premonition shook him. Perhaps he shouldn't

leave Summer alone. He rubbed a kink out of his neck, reminding himself she was with friends, behind locked doors. He was being overcautious. She wouldn't take any chances. She'd be fine.

Chapter Twelve

A few minutes after Summer waved goodbye to Craig, someone knocked on the apartment door. She inhaled sharply, cast a quick glance at the locks, then checked the peephole. Fred stood in the hall, a sheepish grin on his face.

Relieved, she unlocked the door.

"I must have dropped my building key in the bathroom," he said, hurrying across the den.

Gran rolled her eyes at the ceiling and shrugged. "He locks himself out a few times a week. The security guards don't appreciate the extra walk to the back door to allow him in."

As Fred disappeared into the bathroom, the front door burst open. *Now what?* She hadn't locked it behind Fred. With him in the apartment, she wasn't too concerned.

Uncle Bob barreled into the living room, knocked into the couch and staggered. She realized from his wild expression that even Fred might have trouble making him leave. Bob's face was alarmingly red, his eyes glazed.

Summer gagged on the stench of sour wine but saw no cause for alarm. "How did you get past security?"

"Maybe I have a key," he slurred.

Gran scooted the cat off her lap and stood. "No, you don't. Only residents of this building have keys."

Knowing her uncle would never reveal who'd unlocked the door for him, Summer folded her arms over her chest. "What do you want?"

"My stock. You have it and I want my share."

"Oh, piddle." Gran rolled her eyes at the ceiling. "Not this again."

With a shifty look, Bob lurched toward Summer. "You're holding out on me. Just like your mother did. You're not getting away with—"

Bob flung out his arms and lunged at Gran. Summer screamed as the two of them went down in a tangle of arms and legs.

Before she could step forward to help Gran, Fred charged out of the bathroom. His powerful thighs carried him to the middle of the room where Bob sprawled beside his sister, shouting obscenities. Fred snatched a lamp off the table and slammed it over Bob's head. The man collapsed without a sound.

Her heart thumping, Summer knelt by Gran and brushed broken lamp pieces from her hair. "Are you all right?"

"Just peachy. Get the big oaf away from me, and I'll be even better."

Fred grabbed one of Bob's arms and roughly pulled him aside. "I'm glad I came back for my key."

If Fred hadn't returned, Summer wouldn't have unlocked the door, and the problem could have been avoided. After all Fred had done to help, mentioning he'd been as much instigator as savior would have appeared ungrateful. As she searched Gran's eyes, she thought she glimpsed her own reservations mirrored there. However, after noting Fred's concern for Gran, all of her qualms fled.

Bob moaned. Fred's blow had injured him, but not too badly. His limbs moved and he appeared likely to regain consciousness at any moment.

Gran straightened her blouse. With Summer's assistance, she rose to her feet and clutched Fred's arm for support. "Thank goodness you were here, Fred. I don't know what I'd do without you."

"Let's put you to bed," Fred murmured solicitously. "After all this excitement, I think you should lie down."

"That's a good idea."

It wasn't like Gran to be this docile. Normally, she'd be shouting at Uncle Bob and calling security to have her brother thrown into the street. Going meekly to bed just wasn't her style. Either Gran was more shaken than Summer suspected or she was up to something.

Summer peered at Gran's wan face. "Are you sure you aren't hurt? Perhaps we should call your doctor."

"I just need a little rest," Gran assured her testily. "At my age, being tackled just ain't the fun it used to be."

Together, Fred and Summer helped Gran into bed. While Summer tucked her in, Fred brought her a glass of water and her pills. "Here you go."

Gran sipped, then lay back weakly against her pillow. She looked older, smaller, worried. "If you have to leave for any reason, write me a note."

"Sure, Gran. Get some rest. I love you."

"Love you, too."

Summer had no intention of leaving the apartment, but when she returned to the living room, Fred picked up the phone. "I guess you've found your stalker. You want to call the police or should I?"

The stalker? She didn't think so.

Had she been so concerned about Gran, she'd missed the obvious? She turned over possibilities and dredged up Uncle Bob's accusations. He'd accused her of taking the stock, but that was the liquor talking. Although he was about the size and weight of her attacker, many men met that criteria.

As she recalled drinking coffee in his home, sadness overcame her. The man on the floor was nothing like the man who'd defrosted coffee cake in his kitchen. Yet as violent and obnoxious as he'd been today, nothing he'd said convinced her he was the stalker.

"Calling the police isn't necessary. He's just drunk."

"If you say so." Fred put down the phone and rolled Bob to a less awkward angle. As Bob turned, a paper fell out of his pocket. Fred picked it up and tossed it onto the coffee table.

What should they do with her uncle? She didn't want him here when Gran wakened.

She considered splashing water in his face. Then her eyes skimmed the paper. She gasped. Typewritten in the same style as the other notes were the words, "The time is nearing." The note was signed, "The Sentry."

She didn't want to believe it. But the evidence was

right in front of her eyes. Uncle Bob *was* the stalker! She collapsed onto the couch, her stomach churning. She should call Craig, call the police. She couldn't move. Couldn't think.

"What's wrong?" Fred asked.

She handed him the note to read. "You were right. Call the police."

"I'll cancel my tennis lesson. No doubt the police will want us to go downtown. You'll have to give a statement."

CRAIG HURRIED OUT of his office building, pleased with the contracts his attorney had drawn up. While he'd been occupied with Summer, one of his salespeople had brought in a large and lucrative account that would substantially increase their volume. His secretary had found a less expensive way to ship from Singapore that would save thousands of dollars, while a new Taiwanese supplier seemed anxious to give them advantageous credit terms. Business couldn't be better.

He could well afford the purchase he was about to make. The jewelry store he entered was surprisingly crowded with shoppers. Not knowing exactly what he wanted, he took his time, peering into cases glittering with gold and silver. He bypassed the traditional diamond engagement rings. Summer needed something more exotic.

And if they were to continue their masquerade as husband and wife, she also needed a wedding ring. He made his purchases with care and placed the jewelry boxes in his coat pocket.

Eager to return to Summer, he wondered how she'd

react when she saw the ring he'd picked out. When he suggested they make their marriage a real one, he wondered what she'd say. After the way he'd responded to her, his feelings for her must be obvious. She had to know he loved her just as much as she loved him. Finally, the timing was right. And finally, she was ready to hear the words he'd kept back for fear of scaring her away.

Mapping out their future, he drove back to Jarrod's. With the company's increased cash flow, he could afford to hire a full-time bodyguard to protect Summer until they caught the stalker. She could return to law school next semester.

When he knocked on the door of the apartment, Gran yanked the door open. He took one look at compressed lips, hollowed cheeks and drawn features, and his pulse skyrocketed.

"What is it?"

"Summer's in trouble."

SUMMER AND FRED left Bob in custody at the police station. Her uncle had finally come to and insisted he'd never stalked her. He'd even claimed he'd never seen the note.

The worst part was he might really not remember what he had done while he was drinking. Summer still wanted to believe that sober, he would never have put her through the terror of these past months.

She'd tried to call Craig from the police station, but his secretary said he was in the middle of a meeting with his attorney and had turned his cell phone off. Summer felt guilty for all the time he'd missed from his business and, without leaving her name, said she'd call back.

Fred swung off the freeway. "There's something I want to show you."

"What?"

Fred grinned. "The surprise is in the attic of Gran's old house."

"We can't go inside. It's rented. Besides, Gran and I put everything in storage."

"The tenants are on vacation and your grandmother gave me the key. This won't take long."

Apprehension, unexpected in its fierceness, sliced through her. Although Summer had asked a neighbor to look in on her grandmother before they'd accompanied the police to the station, Summer wanted to hear her grandmother's voice reassure her. "Okay, but pull over at a pay phone. I want to make sure Gran's all right and tell her I'll be later than we thought."

Fred did as she asked. While she slipped a quarter into the pay phone, he bought a newspaper, rolled up the newspaper. While the phone started ringing at her grandmother's apartment, Fred walked toward her, striking the rolled newspaper against his palm. His actions jarred her.

With a sense of déjà vu, she recalled the motorcyclist in the park, his baton striking a gloved hand with those exact movements.

Fred was the stalker! Not Uncle Bob.

She needed to run. But the parking lot was empty, the street vacant. Fright made her thoughts race. Fred didn't know she knew. As long as she pretended ignorance, he wouldn't watch her so closely. She could still get away.

"Hello," Gran said.

"Hi, Gran."

Fred's brow creased in surprise and annoyance. "She's awake?"

"Fred's taking me to the old house—"

Fred plucked the receiver from her and slammed it down. He grabbed Summer's arm, his strong fingers giving her no chance to escape. He forced her into the driver's side of the car, shoved her over the passenger seat and climbed in after her.

"Fred, calm down. What's wrong?" She made a stab of pretending ignorance but shook inside at the thought of being alone with him. Little things came back to her. Fred had often been with Gran and her and had overheard their conversations, known where to find her. He could have followed her after one of her visits and she hadn't noticed.

Perhaps while she'd been in Gran's bedroom, he'd planted the note on Bob. It was Fred who'd sliced her underwear, watched her shower, threatened her and the babies.

Craig's babies. Her babies. She had to save their babies.

Fred threw the car into gear and stepped on the gas. "I gave Gran enough pills to knock out a bull. I didn't want her to worry. She should have been sleeping."

He didn't want Gran to worry? What was he thinking?

It didn't matter. She had to concentrate on what to do next. Had Gran heard her say where they were going? Or had Fred cut her off too soon? Would Gran realize anything was wrong?

Eventually, when she didn't show up at the apartment, Gran would remember the phone call. Craig would come looking for her, but by then, it might be too late. She was on her own. If she wanted to escape, she'd have to do it by herself.

Summer considered jumping out while the car was moving. Slowly, careful not to make any big movements, she edged to the door. When he slowed, she'd make a run for it.

Fred's hand clamped onto her neck and he hauled her against him. "Don't even think it. Now that I have you, I'm keeping you."

An ominous shiver froze her bones to ice. She had to keep her wits about her.

"Talk to me. Tell me what you want."

He stroked her neck as if she belonged with him. Acid burned her stomach and she feared she might be sick.

"I want you to honor your promise," he said so softly, so gently, she almost didn't hear.

"What promise?"

"Your promise to marry me." He sounded hurt.

She had no idea what he was talking about. Had he dreamed this up? Or mixed her up with another woman?

"You must have me confused with your fiancée."

"No. *You* are confused. Don't you remember you promised to be my fiancée?" Fred shook his head, his eyes filled with misery. "We played dress-up in the attic. I wore your father's suit and you wore your mother's—"

"Wedding dress." She did remember. He'd asked her to marry him every day for an entire winter when she was six years old. Every day, she'd accepted. Finally, the novelty of the game wore off, and they'd moved on to playing Monopoly and Scrabble.

His voice was triumphant. "So you do remember?"

"We were kids, playacting. It was a game."

He smiled and his voice softened dreamily. "Not for me. I thought you'd dump Kendrick when he couldn't protect you. You were supposed to come back to me. You were supposed to marry me like you promised. Instead, you got knocked up, but we can fix that."

Her stomach knotted into a nauseous ball.

"I love you," he crooned. "I've always loved you. I'm going to love you forever."

CRAIG STRODE INTO Gran's apartment. One quick glance told him Summer was gone. Lamp shards littered the floor and an end table lay on its side as if some sort of brawl had taken place.

Clenching his fists, he spun around to face Gran. "Tell me what happened."

The elderly woman related the events that had taken place. "Summer and Fred had to go make statements."

"They're at the police station?"

She wrung her hands. "I don't think so. Summer called a few minutes ago. She said she and Fred were driving out to my old house."

"Why? She told me it was leased."

"I don't know. We were cut off before I could ask."

"How long ago did she call?"

"Maybe ten minutes. I thought she might call back. When she didn't, I called the police station—she left over half an hour ago."

Summer's mysterious hanging up of the phone and the fact that she had no reason to go with Fred to her old house worried him. Yet those actions might have a perfectly logical explanation.

"I'm going over there. Give me directions."

"WHY ARE YOU taking me to the old house?" Summer's mind raced with panic.

Fred flashed her a grin. "It's a surprise I've been planning for a very long time."

She didn't like the sound of his tone, the sly look in his eyes or the sneaky curl of his lips. She'd suffered more than enough of Fred's "surprises" to last her a lifetime.

But she couldn't escape him before they reached the old neighborhood. The nearby homes would be mostly empty. Gran had raised her in a two-income-family subdivision where most mothers worked to make ends meet. At this time of day, the kids wouldn't yet be out of school. Few people on the street had the luxury of time and energy to play tennis. However, even if a neighbor spotted Fred's tennis whites, his attire wasn't odd enough to cause someone to investigate.

She couldn't depend on outside help. She needed to make her move before Fred got her inside the house. If she hadn't been pregnant, she might have risked jerking the steering wheel and crashing the car into a parked vehicle.

Instead, she looked for a weapon. The car was meticulously clean, and she found nothing useful until her gaze took in the cigarette lighter. She leaned forward, flicked on the radio, tuned to a local pop station until the vehicle flooded with Alanis Morissette's latest hit, then casually pushed in the cigarette lighter.

A vague plan formed. Fred would have to exit the vehicle first. While he did, she'd grab the fiery lighter, jab him and run like hell for the Lightners' house across the street from Gran's. Mr. Lightner *might* be at home.

It wasn't much of a plan. With much of his time devoted to athletics, Fred was in excellent condition. No doubt he could run her into the ground.

But not if he was injured.

She tensed as he pulled into the neighborhood. Nothing had changed much, except the houses seemed smaller than she remembered and closer to the road. They still had oil stains on the driveways, crabgrass in the lawns and toys in the yards. Shingles curled on many of the roofs. Two cats chased a neighborhood dog.

Gran had made a good home for her. Although Summer had lost both her parents, she'd lived a relatively normal childhood. Lots of kids had it worse. Gran had kept her in food and clothes. More important, she'd loved her.

If anything happened to Summer, her grandmother would be heartbroken. And she'd have no one to look after her. A lump formed in Summer's throat. If Craig lost the babies, he might not recover. Thoughts of

Gran, the babies and Craig gave her the courage to fight off Fred. She recalled that people in life-threatening situations could find incredible strength.

Adrenaline surged through her as she steeled herself.

Fred drove down the street. He must have sensed her restlessness. "Take it easy. I know you're anxious to be with me. But I want to drive around the block, make sure no one is watching the house."

"I understand," she said softly, thinking it best to agree, hoping he'd drop his guard.

Summer breathed deeply, readying herself. She'd only have one chance. Her heart pounded like a scared rabbit's, but she tried to appear unflustered as Fred parked in the driveway.

Just as she'd expected, he opened his door and exited the driver's side of the car while maintaining a grip on her wrist and yanking. With her free hand, she seized the red-tipped lighter. Reminded herself to pick the right time, the right target.

Not too soon.

She needed to be clear of the car. On her feet. Ready to run.

Wait.

Wait.

Wait.

Fred held tight to her wrist. As he pulled her out of the car, she hid the weapon at her side and behind the open door. He scanned the street, paying no attention to her. Seizing her opportunity, she jammed the lighter into his bare tanned thigh.

The stench of burning flesh filled her nostrils. Fred

howled in agony, dropped her wrist and clutched his injured leg.

Nerves screaming, heart pounding, Summer bolted for the street.

Chapter Thirteen

Craig's anxiety multiplied during the drive. The more he thought about Summer alone with Fred, the more he pressed the speed limit. Although he'd never suspected the handsome tennis player of stalking, he should have questioned whether Fred had some ulterior motive for assisting Summer's grandmother.

Fred could easily have arranged for the nurse Gran had hired to appear guilty of theft so the old woman would depend only on him. He could have broken into Harry's office and stolen Summer's parents' file. Perhaps he was after the old stock certificates. He'd listened to phone conversations. Knew their plans. From the beginning, Summer had suspected someone at the police department of tracking her movements, but all along, it had been someone much closer to home.

Fred had fooled them all with his fair-haired, tanned, all-American looks. His helpful manner and willingness to please had disguised cunning patience.

Tires squealing, Craig skidded around a corner, swerved past a parked car, a deep, gnawing fear that was almost physical clawing inside him. What did Fred want with Summer? Would he hurt her?

At the thought of losing Summer, he felt a sharp pain in his chest as if a mule had kicked him. He refused to lose another woman he loved.

Falling in love with Summer had helped him reconcile with a past he couldn't change. She and the babies had given him a future again.

Losing her would be intolerable, unacceptable, would shear his heart in two. Summer meant so much to him, but he'd feared telling her might scare her. Or worse, she'd think he was claiming an emotion he didn't really feel because of the babies.

By God, Summer and his children wouldn't come to any harm because he'd abandoned them to sign a business contract. Summer *was* his future.

He had to find her quickly, reassure himself Fred had done no harm. An icy shiver scuttled down his back. He floored the pedal, only easing his speed as he entered a subdivision. The neighborhood left fleeting impressions of one-car garages, concrete-block ranch houses with brick trim and landscaping that had taken root years ago.

He careered around a corner. Finally, he was on the right street. Gran's old house looked like all the rest, faded and worn-out, in need of minor repairs and paint along the eaves.

There was only one difference. A car sat parked in front of it, the driver's door gaping wide open.

SUMMER SPRINTED across the street as fast as her legs could carry her. She didn't dare look back. Didn't have to see Fred's reaction to comprehend the pain in his thigh had only momentarily distracted him from swift pursuit. She forced her legs to move faster. Pumped her arms.

If she could just reach the neighbor's house. Mr. Lightner worked nights. She could wake him. Get some help.

Footsteps pounded behind her, the menacing beat of the chase matching the pulse roaring in her ears. Horror welled up in her. Besides possessing the physical fitness of a conditioned athlete, Fred had the advantage of longer legs and tennis shoes. Despite her head start, his steps sounded right behind her. The heat of his breath seared her neck.

A hand caught her hair, painfully yanked her to a stop. She gasped in agony, couldn't prevent angry tears coursing down her cheeks. She flailed at him with her arms. Kicked his shin. Screamed as loud as she could.

"Stop it!" Impatience frosted his voice as he jerked her against his chest.

When she continued to scream, he wrapped an arm around her throat. Cut off her air.

"Don't make me hurt you. I know you're frightened, but it's going to be all right." His soft, crooning tone contrasted with the hard muscles forcing her back across the street and into Gran's house. The closeness of his body smacked up against hers denied her any further chance of escape.

His words did not reassure her. Nothing would ever be all right again.

When she saw the house's interior, her stomach plummeted. The living-room furniture had been shoved into the kitchen to leave a huge, empty space.

Somehow, Fred had dragged Gran's old freestanding antique mirror into the middle of the room. This mirror had once stood in the attic. They'd posed in front of it. Fred must have removed the piece from storage and transported it here. On the mirror and still in plastic bags from the dry cleaner hung her mother's wedding dress and the navy suit her father had been married in.

"Surprise!" He released her, chuckling happily as if she should be delighted he'd kidnapped her.

The moment he freed her, she spun toward the door. Before she'd taken two steps, Fred slammed the door shut with his palm and cut off her escape.

He shook a finger at her. "None of that." Gleefully, he rubbed his hands together. "I've waited too long for this moment."

Panic flooded her at his crazed happiness. He'd flipped out. Instinct told her to run, hide. Common sense told her there was nowhere to go. She'd never flee through the furniture-filled kitchen to the back door before he caught her again. There was no benefit either to her or the babies in making him angry. He was faster and stronger.

She'd have to be smarter. But what could she do?

"Why did you bring me here?" She tried to keep the rising terror from her tone.

"You are mine. We belong together."

She stared at him, quailing at the implication. Then a renewed resolve flooded her. She'd go along with him for now and watch for an opportunity to escape.

He grasped her hand and led her to the wedding dress. Taking the white satin gown off the hanger, he held it in front of her with cold, assessing eyes and a sad smile touching his lips. "Do you know how long I've waited to see you in this dress again?"

She looked from him to the wedding gown. "I don't understand," she whispered, her voice taut with unshed tears.

"You and I are getting married."

"I'm already married."

He ignored her claim, thrust the dress into her arms and pointed to the bathroom. "Go change." The coolness of his tone hinted at more violent designs. "And don't bother trying to escape through the window. I nailed it shut."

With numb fingers and a shattered heart, she accepted the dress. If he intended for them to marry, he'd have to bring in a minister, a judge or a justice of the peace. Forcing patience, she pretended to yield to him now, but vowed not to give up.

She changed slowly, realizing Fred must have taken Gran's key, removed the clothes and the old mirror from storage in the past few days and brought the items here. After months stalking her, he'd coordinated his kidnapping with the tenants' vacation. Why had he gone to so much trouble? If they were going to marry, the clothes made a weird kind of sense. But why had he taken the heavy antique mirror out of storage?

The oval mirror was big enough to reflect two people from head to toe. The polished mahogany frame was dust free and the faint scent of lemon wax revealed he'd taken special care with the antique. Why was he doing this?

She tried and failed to shake off an ominous feeling. She didn't want to know. Frantic for a way to defend herself, she searched the bathroom for a weapon but found nothing heavier than a shower curtain. The curtain rod wouldn't disengage from the wall without tools. She saw no sign of a plunger.

"Hurry up."

Fearful he'd barge inside if she didn't follow instructions, she hurried into the wedding dress. The off-the-shoulder gown was three inches too short and tight at the bustline, but she managed to do up the zipper.

The instant she opened the door, Fred grabbed her hands. He'd changed into her father's suit.

"What are you doing?" Despite her resolve to remain calm, her voice rose in alarm. For an answer, he whipped a thin cord out of her father's suit pocket. Terror tightened her throat and chest. Overwhelming helplessness struck her. "You don't need to tie me. Please, I'll do what you want."

He hesitated, and a husky note of longing crept into his voice. "When we were six years old, I found a stack of pretty papers in the attic. The borders reminded me of play money."

He looked as if he expected her to understand, but she was completely bewildered. *Just keep him talking.* "*Was* it play money?"

"Of course not. I found the stock certificates." She gasped and he shot her a triumphant glance. "It wasn't until high school that I figured out their value, so I buried the stock under the playhouse. I'd wanted to give it to you as a gift on our wedding night."

She didn't like the way he uttered that last sentence in the past tense. She tried to jerk her hands from his. He held tight, lapsing into tense silence.

She swallowed hard, her knees trembling. "Just tell me what you want. I'll do whatever you say."

Her words elicited no reaction. He just looked at her with big, sad eyes. His strong hands kept her wrists together. She struggled but couldn't break free of his relentless hold or stop him from repeatedly encircling her wrists with the cord.

Anger stirred within her that he'd wrecked her life over a meaningless childhood promise. Drawing a mask of calm over her features, she thought fast. What would change his mind until she could get help? "We could marry and you could still give me the stock as a wedding present."

A fleeting look of pain lanced through his eyes. "It's too late. The money doesn't matter. It would be humiliating to buy your love."

Icy panic engulfed her. All her doubts and fears merged into one loathsome instant of comprehension. He was going to kill her in her mother's wedding dress.

She opened her mouth to scream. He slapped a piece of wide mailing tape over her lips and drew his mouth into a ruthless and grim line.

She fought with all her strength, twisting, elbowing, kicking, until the fear and anger had drained out of her, leaving nothing but a hollow, agonizing void. Despite her efforts, he tied her wrists so tightly her fingers became numb.

Not yet through with her, he dragged her in front of the mirror. Gently, he smoothed back her hair. "As children, we married. We shall become husband and wife again."

Frantic sounds emerged from the back of her throat. If only she could talk to him.

He backed her against the mirror, raised her arms over her head and hooked her bound hands over a post on the frame. He left her on her toes, stretched out, helpless. She tried jumping but had no leverage to lift herself up. Perhaps she could tip the mirror. She tugged hard, throwing her weight into the movement, ignoring the cord slicing painfully into the flesh at her wrists. The heavy mirror didn't budge.

Fred returned from the kitchen a moment later. With a strangely intent expression, he held up a long, thin carving knife. "After we marry, I will send you to Heaven."

His voice sounded normal. His brown eyes didn't look mad, but sorrowful as if he didn't want to kill her. When had Fred become a religious fanatic? If only she could talk to him.

"The angels," he continued, "will watch over you, keep you from running off with other men and having their babies. I know you are a good girl. Death will make you pure." He raised the knife, and she steeled herself for pain. But he set down the weapon and reached for a prayer book, tears in the depths of his tormented brown eyes. "Now we will marry."

She didn't listen as he prayed, droning on and on. If these were her last moments, she wanted to spend them thinking of Craig. Her throat tightened with longing. She couldn't bear that the babies' lives would end before they'd been born. With an agonizing shudder, she shoved the thought aside.

Instead, she recalled Craig's strong arms around her, his wonderful kisses and how much she loved him. She yearned for just one more minute with him to tell him what he meant to her, to tell him how sorry she was they wouldn't have more time.

Fred put down the prayer book. He picked up the knife.

Summer closed her eyes.

CRAIG DIDN'T KNOCK. He kicked in Gran's front door and flung himself inside.

Fred cursed and threw the knife at Craig's head. Ducking, Craig somersaulted, hit the bare floor with a crash and rolled. If not for his quick reflexes, he would have died from the expertly thrown knife.

One glance at Summer in a wedding dress tied to that mirror and Craig exploded with fiery red fury. Before he regained his feet, Fred charged. Locked in a deadly embrace, the two men tumbled across the floor.

Fred jabbed him in the stomach with an elbow. Fire seared his midsection. Craig thrust a knee into his adversary's groin and grimaced in satisfaction as the other man's grip weakened.

"She's mine," Fred shouted. "She's always been mine."

Craig didn't waste breath arguing. He wrapped an arm around Fred's neck. Before he could tighten his hold, Fred back-fisted his temple. For an instant, everything turned black.

Craig's momentary blackout weakened him. Fred wriggled and crawled toward Summer and the knife.

No! He couldn't succumb to the blackness.

A shudder of dark despair tore through him. He had to save Summer.

Drumming up anger, but with only partial vision restored, he lunged after Fred. Missed. Craig's rage smoldered at his failure as he scrambled to stop Fred from hurting Summer.

Fred's hand closed over the knife. He was shoving to his feet with the weapon ready to stab and slice.

God, no! Craig couldn't reach Fred in time to stop him. "Summer!"

White satin flapped. Summer's dress. Uttering a furious grunt, she'd kicked Fred's hand.

Smart girl. Relief flared in Craig as the knife skittered away. She'd bought him another chance.

Craig grabbed Fred's head near his ears. With a gathering of abused muscles and superhuman determination, he twisted Fred off balance, slammed the man to the floor. With an audible crack, Fred's neck snapped. He'd never bother Summer again.

His head ringing, Craig staggered to his feet. He winced at the pain in his side. "Summer, are you all right?"

She nodded vigorously. Joyous tears fell from her eyes.

Effortlessly, he grasped her by her slender waist and lifted her until her hands were free of the post. He set her on her feet and untied her wrists.

She ripped the tape from her lips before she collapsed against his chest. "I never thought I'd see you again."

"I should never have left you alone."

"It wasn't your fault. Fred was...sick." She shuddered. "He expected me to—"

"Shh." He silenced her with a gently placed finger

on her lips. "It's okay. He's never going to hurt anyone again."

AFTER THE POLICE left and the ambulance had taken away Fred's body, they walked outside into the California sunshine. Dogs barked. A woman strolled behind a baby carriage. The normalcy seemed odd after what had just occurred.

"Hold me."

He clasped her shoulders and looked into her precious face. He'd almost lost her. Silently, he vowed never to take her for granted. "You're safe now."

"It's hard to believe. I think it will take some getting used to."

"That's not all you have to get used to." He wrapped his arms around her. "I wanted you from the moment I saw you in black leather. It didn't take long to fall in love with you."

"When did you know?"

A smile teased his lips. "I loved you long before I learned your hair color. Or your name. I love you. I want to marry you." He tightened his embrace. "That's why I was late. I stopped to buy you a ring. When you disappeared with Fred, I thought I had lost you."

She wound her arms around his neck, tilted her head back and looked straight at him. "We have the rest of our lives to sort out details. Kiss me."

And he did.

Epilogue

"I can't believe how much Jason eats," Summer told Craig after their son finished the bottle.

"If you cuddled me that close when I ate, I'd eat a lot, too." Craig stopped digging and leaned on the shovel. His devastating smile pierced her with happiness. With his chest bare, muscles rippling with a light sheen of sweat, and his dark hair slicked back except for one stubborn lock that fell onto his forehead, he looked quite the hunk. He could have posed for bachelor of the year, except for two not-so-minor details. One being his children—Jason, who was cradled in Summer's arms, and his sister, Linda, in a pink lace bonnet, who was cooing happily in a playpen close by.

Two being Craig was already taken. They'd married months before the twins arrived. As she burped Jason, Summer smiled contentedly. She had everything she'd ever wanted. Craig had seen to that.

He'd hired a nanny for the children so she could attend classes. Once she passed the bar exam, she would have a career waiting whenever she chose to accept Harry's offer. But she was in no hurry. The babies were darlings and she didn't like missing too much of their growing up.

She was in no hurry for Craig to finish digging up the ground beneath the playhouse, either. Not when he looked so scrumptious and she had nothing else to do but ogle. Another hour or so of watching him work could be more than pleasurable.

Summer had feared that if they didn't find the missing stock certificates on the first try, the tenants might start searching, so they'd waited until the renters moved out before returning to look for them. Craig had brought her a lounge chair, insisting she nap. But between the squirming baby in her arms and his handsome father, the last thing she wanted was to sleep.

At the sound of a thunk, she placed Jason in the playpen and wandered closer to Craig. "Find anything?"

"Maybe."

Her voice rose in excitement. "I see metal."

He reached into the hole and scraped dirt off a container. "Something's down there." His teasing eyes glinted in the sunlight. "You sure you want me to keep digging?"

For an answer, she reached out and lightly pinched his butt. "Back to work, mister."

"Yes, ma'am. But I *do* earn a bonus for all this manual labor, don't I?"

She raised her brows. "What kind of bonus did you have in mind?"

"I'll leave that to your imagination." Craig went back to digging. A few minutes later, he uncovered an old pretzel can. "Don't get your hopes up. It's rusted through."

Summer kneeled down and eased off the lid. Inside the can was a plastic bag. She handed it to Craig and then dusted off her hands. "You open it. I'm too nervous."

Craig's face remained expressionless as he looked inside.

"Well?"

He grinned. "It's shares of IBM. Over twenty-plus years, the stock has appreciated considerably. I'd say you and Uncle Bob have just become wealthy."

She looked up at his teasing smile, planning just how to give him that bonus after the twins went into their cribs for their afternoon nap. "I was already wealthy. I have the twins, and I have you."

"That's right." He leaned over to kiss her, his eyes glimmering with satisfaction. "And don't you forget it."

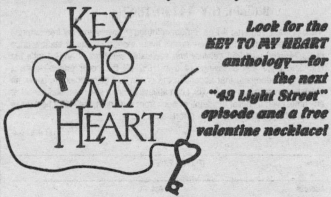
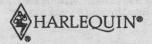

Take 4 bestselling love stories FREE

Plus get a FREE surprise gift!

HARLEQUIN®

I N T R I G U E ®

**There's a small town in New Mexico
where no one is who they seem to
be...and everyone has a secret....**

Welcome to...

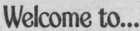

FOUR
WINDS

Join Aimée Thurlo as she takes you to a town of myth
and mystery and introduces you to three men who make
your pulse race....

Meet the Blackhorse brothers—
Gabriel, Joshua and Lucas—in

#427: HER DESTINY (JULY)
#441: HER HERO (NOVEMBER)
#458: HER SHADOW (MARCH 1998)

Come to Four Winds...the town where dreams
come true.

In the mountains of Colorado, the snow comes in on a gust of wind, reaching blizzard conditions in a matter of minutes. Here, the Rampart Mountain Rescue Team is never lonely. But this year there's even more activity than usual for the team, as not only Mother Nature but mystery is swirling in their midst.

Rocky Mtn. RESCUE

Join three of your favorite Intrigue authors for an intimate look at the lives and loves of the men and women of one of America's highest mountain rescue teams. It's the place to be for thrills, chills and adventure!

Don't miss

#449 FORGET ME NOT by Cassie Miles
January 1998

#454 WATCH OVER ME by Carly Bishop
February 1998

#459 FOLLOW ME HOME by Leona Karr
March 1998